GONE

THE COMPLETE SERIES

New York Times & USA Today Bestselling Author
Deborah Bladon

COPYRIGHT

Also by Deborah Bladon

The Obsessed Series
The Exposed Series
The Pulse Series
The VAIN Series
The RUIN Series
IMPULSE
SOLO

GONE

PART ONE

Chapter 1

"I'm looking for Lilly. I have her panties."

I hold my breath hoping that when I turn around that the face attached to that voice isn't who I think it is. It's not that I regularly send men my panties in the mail. Who does that? Okay, I do. I have, but it was just this one time. I admit I regretted it instantly though. As soon as he sent me a picture of himself I wished I had thought it through more. He's hot in a boy next door kind of way. I'm looking for more of a hot in a man who can leave me screaming after taking control of my body kind of way.

"I'm Lilly," I say it quickly as I turn on my heel. "You're Parker, aren't you?"

His deep blue eyes rake over my body, stopping on my nametag. "How do you know my name?"

He's older than the picture he sent me. I'd guess by at least seven or eight years. He has a beard now. His hair is different too. "When did you cut your hair? It's not as curly as I thought it would be."

"My hair?" He pulls his hand through his brown hair before he shakes his head slightly. "I asked you a question. How do you know my name?"

"You know how I know your name or are you acting like this because you got caught?" I lean over the counter and whisper the words softly. "Did you leave your email open and your girlfriend saw that picture you sent me of your..." I nod towards his crotch, which is covered by what looks like an expensive suit. He said he worked in the parts department of an automotive store. Every lie this guy told me online wasn't doing him any favors. If he's looking to hook up he just needs to be himself.

"Caught?" His handsome face twists into a scowl. "What kind of game are you playing?"

"I like to be tied up." I lick my lower lip. "You know about that already."

A ghost of a grin catches the corner of his mouth before it disappears in a flash. "You think you know me, Lilly?"

"I know that you like to do the tying up." I take in a deep breath. Maybe sending my panties to a stranger along with a picture of me nearly naked isn't the worst mistake I've ever made after all.

"Who told you that?" His eyes move down my chest to rest on the top of my cleavage.

He must be one of those types who drinks or smokes weed when he's trolling for pussy online. It makes sense given how mysterious he's acting. I should just ask him if he wants to meet after I'm done with my shift. "What are you doing later?"

"You're full of questions, aren't you?" He places the envelope I sent him on the counter.

I pick it up and pull open the edge. There's nothing inside. "You said you have my panties, Parker."

"I do." He reaches into the pocket of his suit jacket, pulling the edge of the white lace into view. "I told you I have them. I didn't say I was going to give them to you."

I take a step back. I wasn't expecting that. "There's no return address on the envelope. How did you know where to find me?"

His hand dips back into the pocket. My eyes are glued to it. I watch as he slowly pulls a Polaroid picture from its depths. "This was my first clue."

I take the picture from his hand even though I already know exactly what it looks like. I offered to send him a selfie online but he insisted on an actual picture. I'm not one to judge another person's kink so I dusted off my old Polaroid camera, opened up my barista uniform, pulled off my bra and snapped away. "My hair looks good in this." I tilt my head to the side.

"Your hair looks good in that. The rest of you is breathtaking." He rests his hand on the counter. "I like redheads."

"Lucky me," I whisper as I stare at his mouth. His lips are gorgeous. They may be the nicest lips I've ever seen on a man. I'd kill for those lips and those eyes. I get complimented on my green eyes every day, but his are a shade of blue I've never seen before. They're vibrant and deep.

I can't pull my eyes from his face as I hear the bell chime on the door signaling a customer has walked in. If I want to keep this job, I need to take care of that. I'm the only one here.

"I'll be right back." I run my hand over the back of his. "Don't run away."

"Oh, I'm not going anywhere, Lilly." His voice is smooth and even.

I don't take my eyes off of him as I walk back to the cash register. "Welcome to Star Bistro. What can I get for you?"

"Lilly? You're Lilly, aren't you?"

My eyes dart up. I grip the side of the counter. It's him. He's younger with the same curls he had in the picture he sent me. He's wearing a green t-shirt and jeans. He's the one. This is the guy I sent my panties and picture to. "Who are you?" I almost scream the question at him.

"It's me Parker. Don't tell me you don't recognize me?"

"If he's Parker, who the hell are you?" I look right at the suit.

He leans back against the counter, holds my nearly naked picture in the air and points at the guy I've been emailing with for weeks. "I'm his worst nightmare."

"What the fuck?" The t-shirt clad Parker's gaze darts back to me before it rests on the other man's face. "What's going on? Did you text me to come here because you found Lilly for me?"

My eyes volley back and forth between the two men. The color of their eyes is the same. The shape of their noses is identical. Even the shade of their hair is a perfect match. Anyone who took a quick glance at them would be able to tell that they're related.

"I ordered you down here because of this." The suit gestures into the air with my picture still in his grasp. "Why did she send this to my place?"

His place? I hadn't questioned the address I was given by the guy I was flirting with online. When I shoved the picture I'd taken, along with the panties I was wearing, into the envelope, I'd taken it a step further before I mailed it. I wrote a note, detailing how I'd blow him. After signing my first name to the bottom, I'd addressed the envelope with the only name I knew him by, Parker. I hadn't given it another thought, until now.

"She couldn't send it to my apartment." The younger, curly-haired Parker slams his hand down on the counter. "I'm trying to get my girlfriend, Elsie, back. What if she saw it?"

"You can't use my condo for shit like this." The man in the suit barks the words out. "I don't care who you fuck, Parker, but you're not doing it at my place."

"Calm down." He shakes his head slightly causing the bounty of curls that surround his face to bounce, making him look even more youthful than he said he was. He told me in an email that he was twenty-four but seeing him in person I can't gauge how old he is. "It's just a picture."

The suit takes a strong step forward, my picture disappearing into a crumpled mess within his fist. "Calm down? You want me to calm down, you little piece of shit? I come to Boston for the weekend and on the desk in my condo there's an open envelope addressed to me with a naked picture of a redhead I've never seen before."

"So what?" His mouth slides into a half-smile as his hand pulls at the neck of his t-shirt. I can see small beads of sweat on his forehead. "It's not a big deal."

"I had a woman with me." There's no mistaking the disappointment edging the suit's words as he shoves my picture back into his pocket. "She found the envelope before I did. You fucked that up for me, Parker."

It's past nine now which means the bistro is officially closed. It also means I can start my very quick clean-up routine before I lock the front door and take off for the night to find a hole I can climb into where I can hang my head in shame all by myself. Judging by the look on the older Parker's face, I'd venture a guess that unless I step into the middle of this, I'm going to end up watching him pound the hell out of the guy I've been emailing. I've already had enough excitement for one night.

"Hey Parkers," I interject. "The bistro is closed. You can take this outside."

They both turn to look at me and I swear it's as if they just realized I'm still standing here. I should have paid more attention to that quiet voice in the back of my head that told me talking to guys online was a mistake. I should have also listened to my roommate who warned me that sending a naked picture to a stranger would ruin my life.

"Give me back the key to my apartment." The older, better looking Parker's hand jumps out to grab the front of the other's t-shirt. "Now."

The sharp bite of a cell phone's ring breaks the palpable tension in the space. The man in the suit shakes his head slightly before his hand dives into the inner pocket of his jacket, pulling his smart phone out. "Clive Parker," he says calmly into the phone.

Clive Parker? Did he actually say Clive Parker? No, please, don't let him be Clive Parker.

"He's not Clive Parker, is he?" I whisper across the counter to the curly haired guy. "He didn't just say he was Clive Parker."

His eyes scan my face as his brow furrows. "He's Clive Parker. He's my asshole of a half-brother. I didn't know he was until a few months ago when my mom told me who my real dad was and…"

"No," I interrupt hoping that one word will change the reality of the situation. "He can't be Clive Parker."

"He's Clive Parker," he repeats. "I'm Parker Jarvis."

I don't care who he is. His name has no meaning to me. Clive Parker's name does. This is the man whose attention I've been trying to get since I got my college degree three months ago. I've camped outside his office in Manhattan for hours at a time desperately hoping to get a meeting with him. I can't count the number of emails and letters I've sent him filled with my ideas. I've waited impatiently for a response from him but there's been nothing. Now, he's standing less than five feet away from me. The only problem is that he's seen my nude breasts, has my panties in his pocket, and has read my handwritten note explaining exactly how I like to suck cock.

I run my hands over my forehead, trying in vain to get my brain to absorb what's happening. "This can't be real."

"What can't be real, Lilly?" Parker's face is mere inches from mine now. He's leaning so far over the counter that I wouldn't be surprised if he hitched his knee over it to lunge at me. "You need to forget about him. Clive is an ass."

Clive is the one and only man in this world who can give me the future that I want. Everything I've done for the past four years since I graduated from high school has been in preparation of my goal of working alongside him. He has been my inspiration. I glance up quickly, my eyes floating across his handsome face as he talks on his phone. How did I not recognize him when I first turned around ten minutes ago? I've seen enough pictures of him online to know what he looks like. I even saw him briefly from a distance on the street outside his office months ago but he was clean-shaven then. The short beard on his face now threw me off. The fact that he's even more gorgeous close up in person is disarming too. How could I have known that Clive Parker would waltz into the bistro with my naked picture in his pocket?

"Parker," Clive says his name just as he lowers the phone from his mouth. "We're leaving."

"I'm not going anywhere." The playful lilt in Parker's voice is completely misplaced. "I'm going to hang out with Lilly."

"No...um, no..." I stammer as I shake my head violently from side-to-side. "You're not hanging out with me. Not now or ever."

Clive's eyebrow darts up as his eyes shoot over my face. "You're smarter than I thought you were."

That's not a compliment. At any other moment in my life, I'd be thrilled to hear those words coming from his mouth, but not now. Right now, he sees me as a sex crazed girl who chases after men online.

"Clive," I say his name before I realize how out-of-place it sounds. "Mr. Parker?"

His face softens slightly as a small smile tugs at the corner of his full lips. "What is it, Lilly?"

"I'm sorry about this." I offer the words not just as a peace offering. I need to do some major damage control if I hope to salvage the career I've long planned for. "I had no idea when I sent that package that you'd see it."

He takes a step towards the counter, scooping the envelope into his hand. "It's Parker's fault but..."

I cringe as I wait for the inevitable lecture that's about to be thrown directly at me. He's more than a decade older than I am. He's cultured, sophisticated and very accomplished. He dates models and actresses. I'm nothing but a silly young woman who works as a barista to him.

"Lilly." His large hand rests on the counter as he leans forward. "How old are you?"

I pull in a deep breath before I answer in an even tone. "I'm twenty-two."

"You're too young." His words are clipped and simple.

"Too young?" I tilt my head back so I can look directly at his face.

"You're too young to see it now, but you're worth more than this." His chin tips towards the envelope in his hand.

I nod unable to find any words that can refute what he just said. I'm humiliated. I'm devastated and I'm considering running away to another country with the small savings I've accumulated.

"I don't know how many men you're sending pictures of yourself to," he pauses briefly. "I'd suggest you stop it, Lilly. You never know where a picture like this will end up."

I stare in silence as he turns on his heel and walks out the door of the bistro with my picture still tucked in his pocket and my pride spattered all over the floor.

Chapter 2

"If you ask me, you're making a big mistake."

I grin at my roommate. She's quietly watched me all morning as I've printed out my resume, booked a seat on the train to New York City this afternoon and packed a few essentials into my overnight bag. Roni's been my often unwelcome voice of reason since I rented the extra bedroom in her apartment more than two years ago. You'd think by now that we'd call each other friends. That would be a stretch. I realized within days of moving in that she's notorious for waving her wand of judgment at me whenever she pleases. It's never been a secret that she views me as lacking in almost every substantial way. I've learned to ignore her castigating glances and embrace the helpful parts of her. She pushed me through my studies when I felt like giving up. She's become the personal, southern, drill sergeant that I never knew I needed.

"Lilly, are you listening to me?" She plops herself down on the edge of my bed, skimming her hands over the skirt of the cream colored dress she's wearing.

I glance up briefly, my eyes rushing over her face. "I heard you, Roni."

"You've gone down there at least a dozen times." She turns her attention to the unopened stack of mail I have sitting on the desk next to my bed. "You don't actually expect anyone there will see you without an appointment, do you?"

I don't. I can't exactly blurt that out to Veronica Morel, the only person I know who has her entire life organized to the exact minute. I'm flying by the seat of my pants at this point so I offer the one thing I can that will help ease her mind and halt all her incessant questions. "I met the owner of the company last week."

I watch as the furniture catalogue she's mindlessly leafing through falls from her hands. We both stare in silence as it lands with a dull thud on the hardwood floor.

"You met Clive Parker?"

"Yes," I shoot back. "He came into the bistro last Friday night."

"Clive Parker was at Star Bistro?" Her brows rise. "Why didn't you tell me?"

The honest answer to that question is very simple. I'm still reeling from embarrassment over the entire encounter. "We haven't had much of a chance to talk since then."

She leans down to retrieve the catalogue, thoughtlessly pulling on one of the pages. The sheer weight of it rips the corner and it tumbles once again to the ground. "It's kind of a big deal that he was in the bistro, Lilly."

"I know." I don't add anything to the simple retort. I crouch down, tugging the heavy book into my hands. "I'm going to recycle this unless you want it."

She shakes her head briefly. "So you told him about your ideas?"

The question itself would be laughable if it wasn't so disheartening. I'd been trying to secure a one-on-one meeting with the CEO of Corteck for years and the moment that I do have him alone and all to myself, our entire conversation was focused on the semi-nude picture I sent him and my underwear. The lingering knowledge that he read and possibly re-read my handwritten letter detailing how I like to suck cock only made her question about sharing my ideas that much more ironic. "I didn't have a chance but he does know my name now."

"That's a step in the right direction." I sense that she's staring right at me. "Did he invite you to New York to meet with him?"

"Technically, no," I answer truthfully. "He actually picked up something of mine off the counter and I'm going to get it back."

"What did he pick up?"

I pull the zipper on my overstuffed, overnight bag closed. "It's an envelope. It had his name on it."

"Was it one of those letters with your ideas about what you can do for him?" She steps right into the pool of her own assumption. "Do you think what you wrote inside caught his attention?"

The irony of the question isn't lost on me. "I'm sure it did."

"So why are you going all the way to New York to get it back?"

"I wasn't ready to show it to him yet." Yes, I'm referring to the picture of my breasts, but Roni is none the wiser. "I need to explain it more to him so he understands exactly what I can offer him."

If she had any clue about what I'd shoved into that envelope, she'd realize all the hidden innuendo woven into my calculated responses to her questions. Fortunately, she's too focused on her impending date tonight to care what I'm doing or why I'm really going to New York.

***

"You can't just walk in here and expect Mr. Parker to see you," she says rapidly before her index finger darts into the air. It's a silent command for me to be quiet. It's the third time in the past ten minutes that she's used it on me.

I lean forward on the steel counter trying to divert her attention from her call. I had rehearsed what I wanted to say to Clive over and over again last night before I crawled into bed and closed my eyes in a small hotel room near Penn Station. The incessant noise from the room next to mine had kept me from finding sleep. I'm tired, I'm nervous and I'm trying to ignore the fact that this may well be my last chance to get the dream job that I've been pining for most of my adult life.

"Mr. Parker's assistant will call you on Tuesday at ten." She doesn't wait for a response from the person on the other end of the line before she taps a long, bright red fingernail on the phone's base. "I told you to go. Mr. Parker is not in the office today. I'll take your name and give the message to him."

I've played that game for months. I've never had a call returned. Clive has never answered even one of the dozens of email messages I've sent to him. "I saw Mr. Parker when he was in Boston last week. If you tell him Lilly is here, I think he'll see me."

It's more wishful thinking than actual concrete belief. I'm gambling by throwing my name at her. I debated whether or not to do it at length last night. Considering how often Clive Parker is in the gossip pages with a new woman wrapped around his arm, he'd either mistake me for another Lilly or he'd struggle to place the name. I'm betting my entire future on either of those.

"I told you, he's not here." She doesn't shift her eyes from the computer monitor in front of her. "He's out of the office at meetings today."

She wants me to believe her because that's what's expected. I know better though. Three months ago, I had just gotten into a taxi that was pulling into traffic when I saw Clive exit the building. The receptionist then had given me the same song and dance routine. The only difference was that, she, at least, tried to make eye contact with me.

"As I said, I met with Mr. Parker when he was in Boston last week," I pause while I try to search for what I need to say next to get me into his office. "I'm sure he would…"

"You saw Clive when he was in Boston?" The sound of a woman's voice behind me startles me. I turn to look at her. She's tall, brunette, slim and elegant. The smile on her lips radiates into her eyes. This is the first friendly face I've seen since I started my bi-monthly pilgrimage to New York City and the lobby of this building in lower Manhattan.

"I did." I take a step forward. "I'm Lilly Randall."

"Lilly Randall," she repeats my name back as her hand darts into the air between us. "I know who you are, Lilly Randall."

My hand stalls briefly before I clasp hers tightly. I run my free hand over my forehead trying to chase away all the self-doubt. There's no way she can know about the envelope I sent Parker. It's not a possibility. "You do?"

She nods slowly before her arms cross over her chest. "Come with me. We have a lot to talk about."

Chapter 3

"I don't know what I was thinking." She hands me a tall glass of water. "I should have introduced myself in the lobby. My name is Rowan Bell. I work closely with Clive."

I take a small drink. In my haste to get down here by nine o'clock sharp I'd neglected my body's need for food and coffee. I feel parched and the cool water is helping to chase that away. Unfortunately, it's doing nothing for my growing anxiety about how Rowan knows my name. "Thank you for this," I offer before I take another large swallow.

She nods sharply as she lowers herself into the chair next to me in front of her desk. "So you saw Clive when he was in Boston?"

I reach forward to place the glass on the desk before I realize that holding it will occupy my hands so that she won't notice how they're shaking. "We met briefly at the coffee shop I work at."

Her eyes scan me from head-to-toe, taking in the plain navy heels I've paired with a pencil skirt of the same shade and a white blouse. I feel underdressed next to her. I'm not a designer label aficionado by any means, but there's no mistaking an expensive woman's suit when it's sitting across from me, with two very long, perfectly toned legs jutting down to a pair of Louboutin heels.

"You're working at a coffee shop?" She leans back slightly in her chair, her back relaxing. "You haven't pursued something else?"

She's not the first person to ask me that question. It's expected given my drive to get my degree. Software development is my passion but settling for an entry level job where I'm tucked into a cubicle to handle coding errors for the foreseeable future is about as appealing as making lattes. I want one job and one job only and until I know with absolute certainty that I'm not getting it, I'm going to keep my eye on that prize. Crafting beverages and serving sandwiches for a living is only a means to an end. The end is within the walls of this office tower.

I take another mouthful of the water before I look directly at her. "My goal is to work in this organization."

She smiles broadly. "I like your determination, Lilly."

I heave a sigh that I try to hold in. I don't want her to see how incredibly tangled up I am inside. I came here with the fleeting hope that I'd get into the office of the illustrious Clive Parker long enough to not only convince him that I'd be an invaluable asset to his business but also to explain away the package I sent his half-brother. In my scattered thoughts this past week, the panties and Polaroid picture would be my excuse to see him. Once that happened, I'd dazzle him with all my ideas for growth in the app division of his company. It's a convoluted plan at best, but when you're working with the mess that I've made of my life, you can't be choosy.

"I'd really like to discuss some of the ideas I have for…" I start before I abruptly stop. "I mean, I'd like to discuss the possibility of a position here. I know I can bring a lot of knowledge and drive."

She runs her index finger over her cheekbone before resting it against her lips. "You don't have to convince me, Lilly. I'm the one who has been reading all your emails and letters. I can see the potential you have. It's just that we're not hiring right now."

I close my eyes as I hold tight to the almost empty glass that is resting between my palms in my lap. It's what I expected. Corteck has been hovering near the top of the list of the fifty best places to work in North America for the past five years. If a person is lucky enough to land a job here, they aren't going anywhere. I know logically that the chances of me getting hired are slim, but this is the only opportunity I'm going to get to sell myself to someone who has the authority to actually consider me for a position.

"I've had your file in my office for more than a year, Lilly." She leans forward in her seat so she can tap the edge of my knee. "I'll keep it handy. If something opens up, I'll give you a call."

She's expecting me to get up, thank her for the hospitality and exit her office with a smile at the promise of a position that will never materialize. "Is there any chance I can see Mr. Parker?"

"Clive?" She throws me a hard smile. "He's very busy, Lilly. He doesn't handle things like this."

I have absolutely nothing to lose at this point. I can follow the rules and graciously disappear into the crowds of people milling about the streets of Manhattan on this Monday morning, or I can push my luck to its limits. "It's not about this. I need to talk to him about his brother."

Her breathing stalls just as her brow furrows slightly. I can tell that she's trying to regain her composure. "You know Parker?"

I know what Parker's penis looks like. Does that count? "Yes," I offer because it's much easier than trying to explain the sordid details of my unflattering online activity the past few weeks.

"When did you meet Parker?" She runs her index finger over the lapel of her jacket. "You two are close to the same age, aren't you?"

I've always believed that when a person tosses two questions at you back-to-back that you can ignore the first one. It's as simple rule that's always served me well, including right at this moment. "Parker is two years older than me."

"You never mentioned knowing him in any of your emails." Skepticism edges the words.

"I didn't want…" I stammer. "It's just that I didn't want any special consideration because of that."

A faint smile pulls at the edges of her lips. "I understand completely," she whispers as she leans forward. "You want to make it on your own."

Sure. That's it. I'm so far into this hole at this point that I'll grasp at anything.

"As I said, I'd like to talk to Mr. Parker about his brother," I repeat to push the point. "It's important."

She nods before reaching towards her desk to pick up her smartphone. "Clive's not in today. I can relay the message to him when I see him tomorrow."

I sigh heavily. By this time tomorrow, I'll be back at the bistro making some ungrateful customer an overpriced, calorie laden drink with a name that most people can't pronounce correctly. I know that once I walk out of this building, I'll be starting again at square one. "Is there any way I can reach him? I came all the way from Boston."

"Parker's important to you, isn't he?"

No, absolutely not. Parker Jarvis is nothing to me.

I swallow hard. Lying has never come easy to me but this isn't exactly a lie. I shrug my shoulders for exaggerated measure before I answer, "I've shared a lot with Parker."

She stands without warning. Her heels move quickly over the carpeted floor as she rounds her desk. "I didn't realize you knew

Parker that well. I know that Clive has been trying hard to build a bond with him. I'm sure he'd want me to give you extra consideration given that you're a close friend of his brother."

I nod. This meeting has careened into something way more personal than it should be at breakneck speed. I should correct her. I need to tell her that I barely know Parker and virtually every interaction I ever had with him was from the comfort of my bedroom, while I typed out messages to him on my laptop. I don't know anything about Parker other than the fact that he probably has a collection of Polaroid pictures of naked women he's never met and that his dick curves a little too much to the left for my taste.

I lick my lips before I open my mouth knowing that I need to say something. I have to stop this before she assumes that Parker and I are hot and heavy. Who am I kidding? I can tell from the overly wide grin on her face that she's already jumped head first into that theory. "I'd like to talk…"

Her finger jolts up into the air in a gesture that mimics the woman at the front reception desk. It has to be part of the employee training. Her thumb scrolls across her smartphone's screen before she brings it to her ear. "Hi, it's Rowan. I need you to put together an employment package for me." She pauses as her fingers tap the edge of desk. "Do it as an entry level two. Lilly Randall is the name."

I sit silently as I listen to her spell out my name letter-by-letter. This can't be real. I didn't just land a position at the company of my dreams because I sent a random guy a picture of my tits. It may not be my first choice for getting my foot in the door, but I'm in and once I prove I have what it takes to Rowan and Clive, everything in that envelope will cease to matter. It has to. The alternative will mean I'll be making mocha lattes until I retire.

Chapter 4

"Everything is signed." She runs her hand over the edge of the papers. "You can start whenever you want."

Today wouldn't be soon enough. After a woman had knocked on the door fifteen minutes ago with my employment contracts in her hand, I'd fallen into a pit of pure joy. The small details about where I'll live and how much notice I need to give my boss at Star Bistro seem inconsequential right now. Rowan had offered me a temporary position filling in for an employee who was set to start her maternity leave in a few days. I read the fine print and I know logically that the position will only last for three months. I also know that I'm going to make the most of every single hour I'm here. I'll impress them to the point that they won't have a choice but to offer me something permanent. I won't waste this opportunity. I can't.

"I know you have to make some arrangements back in Boston, Lilly." She tucks the papers I just signed into a file folder. "Why don't you give me a call tomorrow and let me know if next Monday works for you."

"Next Monday will be perfect," I shoot back gleefully. "I can't thank you enough for this opportunity."

"You'll fit in well here." She takes a step back signaling for me to stand. "I'm excited to share the news with Clive."

I'm on my feet before his name leaves her lips. In my giddy state I'd forgotten the not-so-small detail of Clive Parker and the fact that he owns the company. My only hope is that he won't put the pieces of the puzzle together and realize that the Lilly that was hired to work on the fifth floor in strategic development is the same Lilly who wrote the detailed manifesto about the best way to suck a man off. By the time he connects those unfortunate dots, I'll have secured my place as a valuable member of the Corteck team.

I volley back and forth on my heels trying to lasso all the nervous energy I feel pumping through me. "I can't thank you enough for giving me this opportunity, Ms. Bell. I promise I'll work as hard as I can."

She races her hand along the sleeve of my blouse, stopping to rest her fingers against my shoulder. "My name is Rowan. You'll call me Rowan and I know you'll do good things here."

I have to. Before the papers arrived, she confessed that she'd have to work some human resources magic to push the person who was supposed to be getting my position into another division. I realize the lengths she's going to help me and I know that it's based primarily on her miscalculating my connection to Clive's brother. With the number of employees that walk through the turnstile in the lobby each day, I doubt that I'll even pass her in the hallway during my time here. I'll quickly become just another payroll number.

"Do your parents live in Boston?" she asks, catching me off guard. "Is this going to be your first time away from home?"

I reach for the edge of her desk to steady my knees. There's no possible way she can understand the tidal wave of emotion that races through me whenever anyone asks about my parents. It's something that I should be accustomed to by now. Friends and classmates asked the same thing on graduation day when I crossed the stage to accept my degree. "I've lived in an apartment near campus for a few years."

She nods and I instantly recognize that the answer matters little to her. She was asking merely as a courtesy. "I'll be in touch tomorrow. I have your cell number."

I take the hint and move towards the open door of her office. "You can reach me at any time. I work tomorrow but I always have my phone in my apron."

"It's been great meeting you, Lilly." She reaches towards me with her hand outstretched. "You're a very welcome addition to our family."

I turn to leave after shaking her hand briskly. I freeze in place, my eyes stuck on the buttons of a crisp, white dress shirt that is covering the chest of a man. I breathe in deeply inhaling the intoxicating scent of expensive cologne. My gaze follows the path of the buttons to his neck, before it rests on his neatly trimmed beard and a pair of blue eyes that I'll never forget.

"Lilly," he says my name in a low rasp. "I'd like a moment."

***

"Would you like something to drink?" Clive asks me from where he's sitting in a leather chair behind his massive wooden desk." I can have my assistant bring you another glass of water or maybe something stronger is in order?"

The glint in his eye suggests that he's testing me. My racing pulse suggests that I'm on the brink of having a heart attack. When he'd asked Rowan for the papers I'd just signed, I saw all my aspirations being handed over to him. I'd silently followed him down the corridor to the bank of elevators and rode helplessly up to the thirty-seventh floor with him knowing that my brief moment of jubilant celebration had crashed into a million non-repairable pieces. My life, as I'd hoped it would be, was no more and it was all because of my stupid need to flirt with some random online.

Way to fuck yourself over, Lilly.

"Lilly?" He leans slightly forward, his elbows catching on the edge of the desk. "Can I get you anything?"

"No," I say sullenly as I try to sink into the chair across from him. There's no way I can hide my embarrassment and disappointment. I feel as though the brass ring I'd always wanted was firmly within my grasp for a mere ten seconds before it was jerked violently away by a gorgeous man who can't take his eyes off me right now. Normally, I'd be flattered by that. It's hard to feel anything but regret and humiliation.

His eyes finally leave me as he leans back in his chair, crossing his legs. "Let's talk about why you're here."

"I was hoping to talk to you," I offer because it's the truth. My initial reason for making this trip was to secure a meeting with him under the guise of explaining why I sent Parker that package filled with erotic delights. I was going to skillfully use that to segue into a discussion about my merits as a potential employee. It's a huge leap but I know if I choose my words carefully, that I'll make my point and convince him that Corteck needs me.

"Why would Rowan offer you a job?" He picks up one of the pieces of paper and tilts it towards me. "Did you bring up Parker's name during your meeting with her?"

I touch my forehead briefly before I trace a path down my nose with my index finger. "I did, yes."

His entire body shifts in his chair. His shoulders push back as his head tilts to the side. "You used your relationship with my brother to get a job here?"

I don't know how to answer that. I did. I didn't do it intentionally but that matters little now. Rowan had made it clear that she had nothing to offer me until I brought up Parker's name. "I just mentioned his name."

"You work at a café, Lilly." He leans forward now, tossing the entire file folder on his desk. "The position you were hired for is highly technical. You're not qualified for it. Is this part of the game you've been playing with my brother?"

I fight the urge to stand and race out of his office. Instead, I slide my ass to the edge of the chair I'm sitting in, I rest my hands on my lap and I say very clearly and calmly, "I'm more qualified to work here than most of your staff. I don't want your brother. I want you."

Chapter 5

No. Wait. I didn't actually say that, did I?

I pull my eyes from the file folder that contains my signed employment contracts to his face. His gaze is set on my lap and where my hands are firmly clasped together. "I'm sorry, Mr. Parker. That came out wrong."

He doesn't acknowledge my words at all. His eyes stay locked on my hands. I move them slightly and that's when I realize. I look down to where my skirt has inched up my thighs revealing the top of my lace garters. I fumble for a moment, teetering back and forth from one ass cheek to the other while I pull the fabric back into place. This can't possibly be going any worse. He has to think I'm an exhibitionist by now. I wouldn't blame him. He's seen more of my body and lacy lingerie than most men I've dated.

"I graduated at the top of my class from MIT," I begin before I stop to cross my feet at the ankles for safe measure. "I've developed several apps that are available in various marketplaces right now."

"You what?" He reaches to pick up the file folder again, skimming over each of the papers. "Why is none of that in here?"

I scoop up my oversized handbag from where I rested it on the floor near my chair and rifle through it. I tossed a copy of my resume and college transcript into it before I left Boston. In my haste to get ready to come here today, I'd forgotten about it. I fish the crumpled mess out of the bottom of my purse. I try to smooth out the wrinkles on my lap before I hold them in the air over his desk. "I brought these."

I see the hesitation in his eyes before he finally reaches to take the papers from me. I can't blame him. Everything about me screams desperate nymphomaniac to him. It's a wonder he hasn't called security to have me removed from the premises yet.

He studies both documents carefully, his brow furrowing as he scans the bottom of my resume where I've detailed the three apps I've developed in the past two years. "This is very impressive. You graduated with honors from MIT?"

I swear that's sarcasm laced tightly into the question. Normally, I'd jump onto a soapbox and rail on the person questioning how a young woman can have the technical knowledge to go shoulder-to-shoulder with male counterparts twice her age. I can't do that now. I have to remember that I'm the one who unwittingly sent him a nude picture. It's no wonder he doubts my academic ability. Smart girls know better than to expose themselves to men they don't know.

"You had a heavy class load," he goes on, "how did you manage to carry that and have time to invest in programming these apps?"

"I love programming." I lean back in my chair. "Two of them began as class projects but I realized their potential so I developed something else for school and focused on these in my spare time."

He straightens his shoulders. "I've had someone dedicated full-time to developing a mobile app that travelers abroad can use when they're faced with a medical emergency."

I pull in a deep breath and try to contain the smile on my face. "As you can see on my resume, I've developed an app just like that but with mine, travelers are able to tell instantly if their insurance will cover their emergency medical situation. They can then easily find a clinic that accepts that insurance based on their current GPS. "

"It's remarkable," he says under his breath.

"I also added a feature that I think is invaluable," I begin before I stall to exhale deeply. "The user can program in all their vital health related information including current conditions, prescriptions, and any primary doctors so that if they're incapacitated at any point, the medical personnel helping them will know what they're dealing with."

"I stare at him waiting for his response. His jaw clenches slightly as he lowers my resume and transcript back onto his desk. "What's really going on here?"

My hand leaps to my cheek. I know my face is flushed. I can feel the heat coursing through me. "What do you mean?" I volley back with little emotion.

"Who sent you here?" He tilts his chin towards me. "You need to tell me right now who the hell sent you here?"

I close my eyes briefly as I try to absorb the words he just threw at me. "No one sent me here. I'm here because I want a job."

"You want a job?" he shoots back. "You tried to seduce my brother and now you're telling me you developed that app all by yourself?"

Wow. Just wow. Asshole alert.

I push my body forward hoping that the action will give me the courage I need to get through this conversation. "Mr. Parker, what happened with your brother was an unfortunate coincidence. I started talking to him completely by accident. I was actually testing out the mobile dating app that your..."

"You expect me to believe that you didn't know who Parker was when you sought him out?" he interjects.

"Sought him out?" I'm on my feet now. "No offense, but your brother isn't really my type."

"Clearly," he growls the word at me as he pushes himself up to a standing position. "Judging by that envelope you mailed to my place, you're willing to do anything to get my attention. It was obvious I'd come looking for you after I got a glimpse of your body."

Was that a compliment? Does it matter at this point? "I sent that envelope to your brother for fun."

"For fun?" he parrots back. "You sent that envelope to my address knowing I would see it. You wrote a letter telling me how you wanted to suck me off."

"No." I want my voice to sound louder than it does but I can't pull anything from within me. "It's not like that."

"What's it like?" he sneers. "It's clear from the contents of that envelope that you were hoping to fuck either me or my brother."

I shake my head so hard that my hair falls into my face. "I wasn't hoping for that. I was only trying to have some fun. It had been a long time since I..." I stop myself. I'm not about to confess that I haven't gotten laid in months.

"A woman doesn't send a man a detailed," he stops to point his finger in the air at me. "A very detailed letter about sucking his dick if she's not looking for a piece of it."

I pull my hands to my face trying to cover up the panic I'm feeling. "I didn't think you'd read the letter."

"You sent a letter to my house about blowing me and you didn't think I'd read it? I want to know right now who sent you, Lilly. Was it someone from Veriolt? Are you working for Taylor

Lungrund? I'm going to find out either way. Make it easier on yourself and just spit it out."

"I have nothing to spit out." It's a poor choice of words given the current discussion, but I'm going to own it. "I'm being completely honest with you."

He's a lunatic. I completely understand now why he's often labeled as difficult and offensive in the press. He actually thinks I'm a spy for one of his two biggest competitors. "I don't know what you're talking about. I've been trying to get a job here for years."

"Bullshit." The word is brutal and direct. "Why haven't I heard about you until now? Explain that to me."

I take a step back out of pure need. I can see the anger within the fine lines around his eyes. His entire face has shifted to a darker place. "Mr. Parker, please."

"Please?" he hisses the word at me. "Please what, Lilly?"

This is it. I have one chance to convince this man that I'm not a mole sent in by one of his competitors to undermine the integrity of his latest developments. "I've always admired you," I say the words even though they sound lame and contrived. "I've applied for the internship program for the past four years and I've written you many emails explaining how I think I can improve things within your organization."

The twisted look of confusion on his face mirrors what I'm feeling inside. That sounded too pompous and expectant. I'm a young woman barely out of college who just told a man who has one of the most brilliant technical minds of my generation that I'm here to do him a favor. "I can verify all these random claims you're making."

I nod briskly. "You should. I mean, yes, please do that."

He leans back against his desk, crossing his legs at the ankles. "I will. In the meantime, why don't you explain one improvement that you'd make today?"

He's pushed me into a corner. The smug expression on his face suggests that he thinks that I'll cave under the pressure of the question. I catch the movement of his brow as he cocks it up.

"Well," he begins as he taps his expensive black shoe on the floor. "I'm waiting, Lilly."

I cross my arms, push my shoulders back and try to contain a small smile. "The dating app you launched three months ago is a piece of shit. The framework is lacking, it has no fluidity at all and the fact that you're charging users for it is a crime."

Chapter 6

"I talked to my father last night about the company that he used to work for," Roni says from the doorway of my bedroom. "It's not exactly what you're looking for, but he thinks he can get you in there doing some coding."

It's a sweet gesture coming from her. Roni hasn't been that supportive of my choice in a career path mainly because she's never understood the appeal of it. She's studying to be a lawyer, a criminal defense attorney, to be exact. "Thanks for asking him about that," I offer even though the idea of moving my life to Alabama to work in a cubicle doing mindless coding forever is even less appealing than working at Star Bistro.

"I'm sorry about what happened in New York, Lilly." She shuffles back and forth on her heels. "You can't blame him for throwing you out of his office after you dissed his work."

Confiding in Roni had been an absolute must after I had taken the train back to Boston yesterday afternoon. When I'd shared my opinion on Corteck's dating app, Clive hadn't reacted in any readable way. He stared at me for what felt like ten minutes before he leaned down to retrieve my purse. As soon as I took it from his grasp he asked me to leave. I had because by that point I knew that it was over. Any hope I had of working alongside him and his team was crushed when I took that Polaroid picture and sent it to his brother. I don't know why I thought he'd ever take me seriously.

"Are you working today?"

I scrub my hand over my forehead before I answer. "I'm doing the late shift. I need to be there by two."

"Do you want to go somewhere for lunch?" Her eyes don't meet mine. "It's my treat."

This compassionate, caring side of my roommate is foreign to me. I already know that I'm not going to be able to handle it in large doses. I need to ease into the idea that she cares about me. "Maybe we can do it another day?" I ask with a small smile. "I'm going to organize some files on my computer."

"Sure thing." I can hear the relief in her voice. Obviously this newfound concern of hers is taking its toll on her as well. "I'm going to run down to the market to get some fruit."

I flip open the cover of my laptop and dive into the task of clearing away all the random projects I've started and never finished the past few months. If I'm not going to get my dream job, I'm going to focus more on developing my own apps. Right now, the ones I do have available are bringing in a few hundred extra dollars each month. I need to increase that tenfold if I want to give up my job at the café.

I spend the next hour organizing my files, saving the important ones on flash drives and tidying up my room. In less than an hour I need to be at work which means now is my chance to have something substantial to eat. I try to avoid the sugary pastries that are brought in for the display case each day. It's a temptation that is often too hard to resist but I'm working on rediscovering the willpower I seem to have misplaced when I started college. I decide on a turkey sandwich on rye and a glass of juice.

Just as I'm settling next to the kitchen table to enjoy my modest feast I hear movement outside the apartment door. For someone studying for a career in law, Roni isn't the most organized person I know. She's dragged me out of class more than a handful of times over the last two years because she forgot her keys in the apartment. I race to the door to let her in, knowing that she likely bought way more groceries than either of us will be able to consume in a month's time.

"You can thank me later for rescuing you," I say with a smile as I swing open the door.

"I'll thank you now." His mouth curves into a grin as his eyes skim over the red boy shorts and tank top I'm wearing.

"Mr. Parker?"

"Lilly Randall." His voice is deep and seductive. "Aren't you going to invite me in?"

Chapter 7

"I wasn't expecting you," I mutter as I walk back into the main room after excusing myself to get dressed. I pulled on a pair of jeans and a black sleeveless turtleneck sweater before freeing my long red hair from the ponytail it's been in all morning. "I don't normally answer the door like that."

"I should have called first." He turns from the bookcase he's been standing in front of for the past few minutes. "I was at MIT and decided to take a chance that you'd be home."

"You were at MIT?" I don't even try to veil the surprise in the words. I'm still reeling from the shock of seeing him standing in my doorway. Add to that the sheer horror of again revealing my underwear choice to him, and it's a wonder I didn't climb onto the fire escape outside my bedroom window. I don't want to jump to the conclusion that he was at my alma mater to confirm I graduated from the computer science program with honors. I'm hopeful that was part of his visit though.

"I had business in Boston today," he stops before he corrects himself. "Personal business and I thought I'd stop in there and catch up with an old friend."

The fact that he's talking to me at all isn't lost on me. "Why are you here?"

"I spoke to Rowan after you left yesterday." He pulls on the fabric of the pants covering his thighs before he lowers his tall frame into a beige rocking chair. "She showed me some of the emails you'd sent to us over the years."

I had hoped for a very brief moment in time on the train ride back to Boston that he'd discuss me with her. The optimistic part of me wanted to believe that she'd convince him that my technical ability trumped everything else. The more realistic part of me knew that she'd likely tell him that I used my brief encounters with Parker to get my foot in the door.

By the time I finally got off the train after the three and half hour ride, I felt despondent. I'm not a foolish person. The knowledge that I may have lost the promise of a fulfilling career because of a mistake I made online is devastating.

"Have you spoken to Parker at all since you saw him at the bistro?" he asks softly.

I shake my head faintly. "No. I don't have his number and I haven't emailed him. I regret what happened with Parker."

"How did you initially connect with him?"

I swallow hard. It's not a question that has a simple answer and it's going to bring back to the surface a topic I'd rather keep buried. I can't avoid it though. If he hasn't already asked Parker about it, he will. I need to bite the bullet and spit out the truth. "I was testing out your new dating app when Parker contacted me on it."

"The mobile app? The one you think has flaws?" His tone is hard to decipher. I can't tell if he's still offended by what I said in his office yesterday morning. He's had more than twenty-four hours to absorb my brutally honest critique of one of the biggest launches in his company's history.

"Yes," I offer back in a hushed tone. "I thought that if I used the product, I'd be able to offer some viable suggestions in terms of improvement. I was hoping that would get me a meeting with you."

He traces his index finger over his bristled jaw. "I asked Parker to use the app. I've been trying to get him involved with the company."

I nod even though this is the first I've heard of it. I assumed that Parker was just a guy on the prowl. "We decided to switch over to email because it was easier for him."

A faint smile runs over his full lips. "Parker told me that he had trouble with the app."

I feel a sense of validation at the words. It's not likely that his brother's opinion will help to substantiate my brutal view of the app, but it certainly can't hurt. "I didn't know who Parker was at that time. He seemed fun and nice."

For the first time since he walked into the bistro last week, I sense understanding in Clive's eyes. "Parker's life is a mess. His history with women is complicated. I'm glad you didn't get too invested in him."

It's the words that you'd expect from a close friend who has your back. "I got caught up in the things we talked about. I don't think I'll hear from Parker again."

"You're right about that." Grinning, he taps the arm of the chair with the palm of his hand. "I put Parker on a plane to Dubai this morning. He'll be working at our division there for at least the next two years."

Chapter 8

Note to self: don't piss off Clive Parker or your ass will be shipped off to a remote location for the foreseeable future.

"Rowan said that you'd be available to start working for us next week." His eyes don't leave the screen of his smartphone. "Does that still work for you?"

"You want me to work for you?" I ask because I need to fully grasp what he's saying. In a span of a little more than twenty-four hours I've gone from burying any hope I might have had of working for his company to hearing him asking me if I'm ready, willing and able to take on the task.

"You've already signed all the necessary paperwork." His eyes flit over my face at a rapid pace. I can tell that he's not eager to dredge up what happened in his office yesterday.

"I just assumed after our discussion yesterday that it wasn't going to happen."

He rests his phone on his thigh, his eyes jutting up to meet mine. "I want to apologize for what happened in my office. I work in a cutthroat industry, Lilly. We've had several issues in the past of employees sharing sensitive information with our competition."

I know it happens. It only makes sense given the drive to always have the upper hand in the field of technology and gadgets. There had been several stories in the news about lawsuits leveled against employees of Corteck. I assumed that's why I had to sign a non-disclosure agreement in Rowan's office yesterday. I had done so without question. "I understand, Mr. Parker."

He leans forward, pulling his phone into his palm. "Do you have a place to live in New York?"

I don't. My intention was to hit the ground running on that today. I was going to look into an extended stay hotel until I could find a more permanent solution. "Not yet. I can start figuring that out today."

"A friend of mine is looking for a roommate." He stares directly at me, his blue eyes looking even more vibrant in the natural sunlight that is streaming in through the window on the wall directly behind me. "You'll be able to easily afford it on your salary and it's only a short subway ride from there to the office."

"That sounds great," I offer back trying not to sound as utterly shocked as I feel. "That would help me out a lot."

"I'll have her contact you." The edges of his mouth soften.

"Thank you." I smooth my hands over the legs of my jeans. "I'm excited to start working for you."

"I want to clarify something, Lilly." He scrubs his hand over his forehead. "This is uncomfortable, but necessary."

I flinch not only from the words, but also from the expression on his face. "What is it?"

"You're a very attractive young woman." He tilts his chin upward so his eyes catch mine. "You're obviously very comfortable with who you are."

I swallow hard. I can't tell if he's waiting for me to confirm that or not. "Yes," I say quietly because I can't think of anything else to fill in the silence that is now enveloping the room.

He blows a puff of air out between his lips. "I need you to understand that I prefer if my employees keep their personal lives out of the office."

I feel my shoulders heave forward involuntarily. Why wasn't I expecting this lecture? The man sees me as a nothing but a horny, half-naked fool. I cast my eyes down. It's a label I'm never going to be able to drop. He'll always view me as the redhead who showed her tits off to his brother. "I think I understand."

"You're going to be working in a division that is primarily men." He taps his finger on the arm of the chair. "You're going to be propositioned a lot."

I raise a brow. "I can handle myself."

He counters with a cock of his own brow. "I have no doubt that you can handle a lot, Lilly."

"I'll keep things professional, Mr. Parker." I dart my tongue over my bottom lip.

His eyes lock on my mouth before his own tongue traces a slow path over his top lip. "Keep it professional in the office. What you do after five o'clock is up to you."

***

"It's almost five o'clock. You need to live a little." He's trying to coax me to give in.

"A cocktail party in the office?" I turn my head to look at Dan, one of the men I met four days ago when I started working at Corteck. "Does that happen a lot?"

"A few times a year." He crosses his arms over his chest. "It's a mixer so new employees can meet us lifers."

I laugh at the inference that Dan is a lifer. He's the one person I've spent the most time with since I walked through the door of the building earlier this week. He's helped me set up my computer, he's shown me around the offices and I've heard countless stories about how blessed he is to have the most amazing wife, children and grandchildren in the world. In a very short period of time, he's become someone I can count on to help guide me through the maze of my new job.

"You're going to be there, right?" He taps the face of his watch. "It starts in a few minutes in the conference room on the twenty-eighth floor."

I want to ask if Clive will be there. I haven't spoken to him since he walked out of my apartment last week after telling me I had free rein to fuck whoever I wanted after work each night. He might not have used those exact words, but there was no mistaking his body language. I saw the same glint of desire in his eye when he first walked into the bistro. The problem is that he's my boss now, and judging by the murmurs that I've heard floating through the air at the coffee station and in the lunch room, the man has a type and that's anything that struts down a runaway and is near six feet tall. I'm ten inches too short and I program computers all day. I'm beginning to think that what I saw in his eyes was nothing more than amusement.

"Do you think I have to go?" I tap a few keys on my keyboard. "I'd rather stay here and work."

"Working late isn't going to get you anywhere, Lil." Dan walks over to my desk. "You need to mingle. Most of the division managers are going to be there. "

I suppose that should mean something to me. "I don't see how that matters. I'm here for three months."

He pushes on the corner of a piece of paper on my desk. "Division managers can make whatever changes they want. If you hit it off with one, you might get something long term."

I scratch my ear. "I hadn't thought of that."

"You need to start seeing the big picture." He holds out his hand. "We'll go together for an hour tops and then we can both take off."

I study his palm. "Just an hour?"

"I'm taking my wife out for dinner." He fumbles with the one button on his dress shirt that always pops open over his stomach. "I can't disappoint that woman so I have to leave in an hour."

"I can do an hour." I push my hands against my desk and pull myself up. "I'm ready if you are."

Chapter 9

"Everyone has rules when it comes to who they'll fuck." An obviously excited man's voice carries over my shoulder.

I've never been at an office cocktail party. We didn't even have a holiday party at Star Bistro so this is a new universe for me. Who knew that the uptight people I work alongside all day would become so open and willing to discuss their sex lives once they had a glass or two of wine? I glance down at the half full goblet of red in my hand and decide that I've reached my limit. If I keep up the pace with my co-workers I'm going to start sharing details about what I like to do in bed.

"What are your rules, Lilly?" Kathryn, a woman I met mere moments ago breathes down my neck. "It's different nowadays, isn't it?"

All eyes in the tight group of seven I'm standing in are locked on me. I'm not a prude. The renowned Clive Parker himself can attest to that. I'm just not that willing to share intimate parts of my life with these people. I have to come back to the office on Monday morning and I want to be able to do that without any stigma attached to my face.

"When I was your age we waited until we were married before we did a man." Kathryn is on a roll and I'm right in the path of that. "You've probably done more guys this month than I've ever done."

Way to throw me under the whore bus, Kathy. "I doubt that," I say back because, seriously, what else is there?

"Just tell us your rules." She taps her hand on my shoulder. "Do you like them younger, or older?"

I'm not getting out of this without at least a few questions answered and this one is easy so I'll go for it. "I don't have a preference when it comes to age."

"That's great news for me." Bernie, who I'd venture to guess is nearing retirement age, adjusts the bow tie around his neck. "We could take this party to my place, Lilly."

Or I could hide under the table near the entrance where two women are happily pouring drinks. I laugh only because I can't think of a retort that wouldn't be biting. I'm trying to establish more business relationships here, not land myself in the bed of a man old enough to be my grandfather.

"Clive has a thing about age." Kathryn's voice is back in the mix. "I've heard rumors about it."

I actually wonder for a brief moment whether the back of my ears perked up at the mention of his name. I've taken extra time in the lobby and in the hallways all week hoping to run into him. I've never met a more attractive man and as of right now, his face and body are what I'm imagining when I'm standing in the shower of my new apartment every morning making myself orgasm.

"What rumors?" Bernie leans closer to me as if I'm the holder of that secret. "Does he like them as young as Lilly?"

I shouldn't be as invested in the answer to his question as I am. I wait for Kathryn to pipe up and spill the goods but there's only silence in our corner of the room.

I fidget on my feet before I realize that everyone's eyes have shifted to a space near the entrance to the conference room. I turn to follow the line of their gaze and there he is. Standing at ease in a dark suit, blue shirt and a small grin on his face is Clive Parker.

"He's so fucking hot," Kathryn whispers into the air. "I'd cheat on my husband for that."

I lift my hand to my mouth to stifle the laugh I can't contain. It's what every woman in the room must be thinking judging by the way all female eyes are following every step he's taking.

"He's coming over here," Bernie announces even though no one has stopped staring. The entire room has gone quiet.

I pull the wineglass up to my mouth. I don't give it a second thought as I push it against my lips and down it in one quick swallow just as he stops next to Kathryn.

"Is everyone having a good time?" His voice is cultured and refined. There's a playful lilt in his tone that I haven't heard before.

"Your parties are always the best, Mr. Parker." Bernie tips the short glass of amber liquid in his hand towards Clive.

"I'm glad you're having fun, Bernie," Clive says the words through a smile although his gaze is locked on me. "How about you, Lilly? Are you enjoying your first mixer?"

I nod slowly. "I am."

His eyes sweep over my body, soaking in the green shift dress I'm wearing along with black heels. "I'd like to see you in my office."

My heart stops. I literally feel it stall within the confines of my chest. "Now?"

"If I can tear you away from this, now is perfect."

Chapter 10

It's almost seven o'clock. That means that I'm free to do what I want according to Clive Parker's rules. That would be more exciting if I wasn't stuck in the middle of a meeting I don't belong in.

My eyes travel slowly over the handsome face of Clive's assistant, Bruce. He's slightly older than I am. By first glance one would think that he's happy to be here late on a Friday but the scowl that took over his expression when Clive turned his back to him made it clear there's more than a small bit of hostility there. I haven't heard much about Bruce since I started here, other than the fact that he worked his way up in the company to become Clive's right hand man.

He was gracious to me the moment I walked through the office door on Clive's heel. He'd offered me something to drink almost immediately and the tender way he said my name helped volley my mood.

It's a stark contrast to Clive who hasn't said more than two words to me since I followed him out of the conference room. I'd spent the entire elevator ride to the floor that houses all of the corporate offices, listening to him talk football scores with a man my age. I honestly was having more fun at the mixer and I'm beginning to feel a bite of resentment for being pulled out of that.

"I need you to firm up my itinerary for London next month." Clive's eyes don't leave his tablet's screen as he continues with the never-ending list of things he wants Bruce to take care of. "I'll need to have that on my desk on Monday."

"I'll have it ready by tomorrow." Bruce taps something into his smartphone. "Is there anything else?"

I've heard him ask it at least three times since we walked through the office door almost thirty minutes ago. I've occupied myself by sitting patiently on one of the chairs near Clive's desk clearing all the old messages out of my phone.

"I think that's it." Clive finally stands and I'm tempted to do the same. "I'll see you out."

"I should probably be going too." I toss my phone back into my purse.

"You'll sit right there until I get back, Lilly."

"It was nice to meet you." Bruce throws me a look that screams of quiet understanding. "I'll see you around the office."

I nod as I try and pull a small smile to my face. I lean back, rest my head against the luxurious leather and settle in for whatever Clive has in store for me.

***

"It's a beautiful city, don't you think?" His voice is barely more than a whisper as it edges over the back of my neck. "I love New York."

When he didn't return immediately, I'd walked to the bank of windows that overlook the darkened city. I stood in silence, focused on the many people moving along the sidewalks. I hadn't noticed his reflection in the window as he approached me. Now, he's almost touching my back. "It's a wonderful city."

I feel him step forward a touch and out of a need to keep my composure I do the same. I look down when I realize that the toes of my shoes are touching the floor length window. I breathe out so heavily that my breath clouds the glass.

"Are you enjoying your time here, Lilly?"

My hands shift restlessly in front of me. I have no place to put them. I clench them together tightly as I answer the question in as calm a voice as I can. "This is a wonderful place to work, Mr. Parker."

I jump slightly as his right hand juts past me to rest against the glass of the window. "You're working here now. You can call me Clive."

"Clive," I repeat back realizing how misplaced it feels on my tongue. In some abstract way I enjoyed the formality of our exchanges.

"Say it again, Lilly." The words leave his mouth just as his left hand leaps to the glass, trapping me within.

"Clive," I say in a breathless whimper. I look up to catch his gaze in the reflection of the window. "I'll call you Clive."

"What were you talking about in the conference room when I walked in?"

The question is ripe with hidden innuendo. He must have seen the anxious anticipation on my face when he first spotted me across the room. There's absolutely no way he can know that Kathryn was about to tell me the age of the women he likes to fuck.

"Nothing." I try to smile. "It was nothing."

"I've been to those mixers for years." He leans closer to me. "I know what Kathryn likes to talk about."

I can feel the outline of his erection against me. He's as aroused as I am. The scent of his skin, combined with the position he's trapped me in has me more desirous than I've ever been. I fist my hands at my side to try and avoid the yearning to twist around and wrap them in his hair before I pull him into a deep kiss. "She's very friendly."

His head roars back with laughter as he briefly grinds himself into me. The motion catches me off guard and I'm certain a small moan escapes my mouth. He stops abruptly and stares at my reflection in the window. "Did Kathryn tell you she'd like to fuck me?"

My lips part slightly. I run my tongue over them trying to chase away the desperate need I feel to push my body back into his. "I don't want to get her into trouble," I say with no sincerity at all. I don't care if Kathryn has a job on Monday or not. I do care if I have a job and right now I can't tell if Clive is testing the limits of what I'll do to keep it or not.

"It's almost eight now, Lilly." His right hand drops from the glass onto my thigh. "Do you remember what I told you about what happens after work?"

I push my hands against the glass, resting my forehead against them. "Yes, but..."

"Kathryn told you that she wants to fuck me. Kathryn has told everyone that she wants to fuck me, including me." A deep rumble flows through his chest and into me. "The woman has made it very clear that I have an open invitation."

I gasp when I feel his hand skim the hem of my dress.

"I've dated a lot of women." His lips are floating over the tender skin of my neck. "I've fucked most of those women."

I pull my head away from the window so I can watch his hand in the reflection. My eyes are glued to it as it continues to slide up my thigh. "Mr. Parker...Clive...I" I stammer because any words that might have been ready to come out are now caught on the tip of my tongue.

"I've never met anyone like you." His fingers run hot over the edge of my lace garter. "You almost had me on my knees when I saw this for the first time."

My eyes dart down as I feel his hand move higher still. "Please," I say through a moan.

"Lilly." His lips touch my neck in a soft kiss as his index finger brushes over my inner thigh. "Spread your legs for me."

I don't hesitate as I push my hands against the glass and edge my feet apart. I want to say something. I should say something but the overwhelming need my body has to feel pleasure from his is silencing everything but my want.

"I've thought about how beautiful your breasts are since I saw that picture of you." His voice is heavy and slow as he wraps his left hand around my waist, pulling my hips into him. "I haven't stopped thinking about what your cunt looks like. How pretty and pink it must be."

I've never heard that word fall from a man's lips so effortlessly before. It's filled with crude, measureless desire and it pulls a small uncontrollable moan from within me. "I want…"

"Everything your body wants, I'll give to it, Lilly." His long fingers slide over my silk covered mound, pulling the wetness into the fabric. "You're so wet."

I push back with my hands still resting against the glass. The city below us hasn't stopped at all. No one passing by the building in a rush would know what was going on against the window, stories above where they are. The office building across the street still has a sprinkling of lights on and I suddenly realize what that means. "Can anyone see us?"

His index finger quickly dives beneath the edge of the leg of my panties and I almost cry out from the sudden rush of sensation as he hones in on my swollen clit. "You wax. I knew that you'd wax."

My right hand falls from the glass to my crotch. I want desperately to feel more so I press my hand over his; the only separation of our skin is the silk of the fabric. "I like to be smooth."

"Fuck," he growls into my neck. "Spread more for me."

I lean my hands against the window knowing that I need the leverage if I'm going to shift position at all. I'm close to an orgasm already and it's not just from the perfect, skilled pressure he's applying to my core. It's the sound of his voice and the smell of his skin and the dangerous edge of knowing that someone could be gazing past the corner of one of the closed blinds in the building across the street. I slide my right foot over before following suit with the left. I swallow hard to stifle a scream the moment I feel him slip his finger into my channel.

"You're going to come for me." His lips are against my cheek now, his free hand wrapped around my neck. "I want to hear the sweet sounds you make when you come all over my hand."

I lean back into him, giving in to my body's need to find its release. I grind my hips into his hand, seeking more depth of pleasure. "Touch my clit. Please, Mr. Parker. Touch it."

The only sound that fills the room is the low growl that flows from him as he pulls my clit between two of his fingers, leading me closer and closer to the edge.

"I'm going to come," I say breathlessly into the air.

He tilts my head back by the slight pressure of his hand on my neck as he glides his lush lips over mine. "Let me hear it, Lilly. Let me hear it."

My knees buckle as the orgasm hits me with brutal force. I whimper softly before I let out a deep, guttural moan.

Chapter 11

"Mr. Parker?" A woman's voice calls from the doorway of his office.

I panic because that's what women instinctively do when they're caught in a compromising position with their boss. I try to push free of his embrace, but he grazes his moist lips over my cheek before he lets go of my neck and pulls his hand free of my panties.

"Don't move." His breath whispers over my ear. "Stay right here."

I'd do as I'm told but the parts of me that believe I should run out of his office with my face covered by my hands are winning the internal battle that is going on within me. I have no idea how long the woman at the doorway has been there. I don't know what she heard or saw, but I do know that I'm not about to stick around to find out.

I turn quickly only to look up to the calm and very relaxed face of the man who just gave me a mind-numbing orgasm. He bites the corner of his lip before he slowly brings his hand to his face, running two of the fingers that were just buried within me across his mouth. I watch in silence as he shifts the position of his hand. I understand immediately when he holds his index finger in place over his lips. He wants me to be quiet. I need to do that.

"Allison, I'm busy." He pivots so he's facing her now. "What do you want?"

She twists her lips into a grimace before she teeters back on one of the black stilettos she's wearing. "You asked me to meet you here at eight. It's eight."

I stare at the back of his head as it dips towards his wrist and the silver watch adorning it. "I forgot we had a meeting."

"You asked me to meet you here." There's no disguising the disappointment in her tone. "I moved another engagement so I could do this."

"I need to go." I move from where I've been standing in silence behind him. "I should get home."

He catches the skirt of my dress before I have a chance to take even one step forward. "Lilly, I'd like to talk before you leave."

My eyes volley from his face back to the woman's at the doorway. I recognize her from a few photographs I've seen online of her and Clive together. She heads one of the many charities that Clive dedicates his resources to. Her arms are crossed and I can sense that she's feeling just as uncomfortable as I am. I may have been the one pressed into the window getting fingered to an orgasm, but she had to witness the aftermath of that. I can't even entertain the thought that she watched the entire thing, so I'm going to assume that based on her somewhat calm demeanor that she didn't see much more than Clive's arms wrapped around me.

"Are you going to have time to meet with me or not?" Allison takes a step into the office. "I'd like to be done this by midnight."

I follow her cue as I pull gently from his grasp. "I need to go."

He doesn't try and stop me. He only nods in agreement as I watch him slide his suit jacket from his shoulders. I start to walk out but before I cross the threshold I turn one last time to see him sitting next to her on a white leather sofa resting against a wall adjacent to the window. His arm is draped lazily over the back of the piece of luxurious furniture as he talks quietly to her. I step away from the doorway the moment I see her rest her hand on his knee.

***

"Have you ever slept with your boss?"

Rebecca bites the corner of a piece of toast. "Clive is your boss. Are you fucking him?"

I obviously didn't think this conversation through. "No, it's not about me."

"No one believes anyone who says that, Lilly." She takes a bigger bite of the dry bread before chasing it down with a swallow of coffee. I instantly hit it off with her in a way I never had with Roni. Rebecca welcomed me with open arms and gave me a primer on what to expect when it comes to dating men in Manhattan. She's a few years older me, but there's a big sister aura about her that I'm already crazy about. Having her for a roommate is giving me a sense of belonging I haven't felt in a long time.

"When did you meet Clive?" I ask not out of any real curiosity. I'm simply trying to steer this disaster of a discussion into a place that takes the spotlight off of me and what happened in Clive's office last night.

"It was months ago." She presses her index finger between her lips before pulling it over the plate. She licks the scattered crumbs of the toasted bread from her skin. "It might be close to a year now."

"How did you meet?" I pour myself another cup of coffee before topping off hers. "Did you work for him?"

"No." She tips her chin towards the mug. "Can you grab the milk out of the fridge for me?"

I take a step to the left and open the refrigerator door wide enough to pull out the small carton of milk. "Did you date?"

After pouring a heavy dose of milk into her mug, she pushes the carton back to me. "I was dating someone when we met. We hit it off as friends right away."

Somehow the idea of Clive Parker being friend zoned by a woman as beautiful as Rebecca seems almost impossible. "He said you two are good friends."

"He's been my go-to guy when I have real guy trouble." She giggles at the implied inference that Clive isn't a real man. "He's helped me a lot with dating stuff and life stuff."

"It's great to have a friend like that," I offer out of courtesy. I've drifted away from most of the close friends I've had in my life. It's a hole that I'm hoping I can fill now that I'm beginning to settle into life in Manhattan.

"I used to have this friend named Jess." She points towards the hallway. "She actually lived here when she first moved to New York from Connecticut."

"In my room?" I ask.

Her nose wrinkles slightly. "It was her room. It was one of the best times of my life. We had a lot of fun together."

"Did you fall out of touch with each other?"

Her eyes flit over my face quickly before she pulls them down toward the counter. "I got in the middle of her relationship and things went sour."

"That's rough." I want to reach out to comfort her but I've known her for less than a week. "Maybe you can repair things one day."

"I've tried." She picks up the mug in both her palms. "I actually met Clive when I went to see Jess at work one day."

"Does she work at Corteck?"

"She's a chef. She works at the restaurant that Clive's nephew's adopted father owns." She tips her chin with each reference. "I think I have that right."

She does have it right. She's talking about Hunter Reynolds, the man who owns both Axel NY and Axel Boston. He's the adopted father of Clive's nephew, Cory. Cory was named after Coral Parker, Clive's sister who died more than a decade ago. There's no shortage of information online about the tragedy of Coral's death and her family's decision to donate her organs. Her heart had been transplanted into Hunter Reynold's wife, Sadie. It's a cruel twist of fate that I found not only fascinating, but also heartbreaking.

"Clive could see I was in pain," she continues without any prompting from me. "He's lost a lot of people in his life, so he understands."

I understand too but pushing my past into this conversation isn't going to happen. Not today, and maybe not ever. I've rarely shared with anyone what happened to my parents and judging by the pain that Rebecca still seems to be in over losing her best friend, I don't view her as a sympathetic shoulder I can lean on.

"I'm here if you ever want to talk." I tap her hand before I reach for the milk to tuck it back into the fridge. "I need to take off."

"Where are you going so early on a Saturday?" she calls after me as I pull a sweater over the simple white dress I'm wearing.

"The library," I toss back as I yank my apartment keys into my palm and head out the door.

Chapter 12

"Where does a young woman new to the city spend her Saturday?" Clive asks, his voice sounding husky.

"I'm at the library," I whisper into my phone not wanting to draw any attention from the other patrons who are gathered around trying to read or study.

"The library?" There's a pause and I hear the unmistakable rustling of sheets. He's in bed. I glance down at the corner of my laptop screen. It's after one in the afternoon. A sudden ache pours through me as I think about what it must be like to spend a lazy Saturday morning tucked into Clive's bed and his arms.

"I'm catching up on emails and stuff." I don't elaborate because there's no need to. I'm not on his company's time at the moment. It's the weekend and I'm free to do whatever I want until I step back into the lobby of his building on Monday morning. Until then, my time doesn't belong to him.

"Have you had lunch?"

It's a question that catches me completely off guard. When I first saw his number calling me, I assumed he wanted to explain away what happened in his office last night. I had tossed and turned for hours after going to bed reliving every touch of his hands on my skin. "Not yet."

"I can be ready in fifteen."

The casual way he says the words surprises me. I've never imagined sharing a meal with him. "Do you want me to meet you somewhere?"

"You took the subway to Fifth Avenue, right?"

It's not surprising that he'd jump to that conclusion. Stepping into this branch of the library was like entering another world. The striking architectural details only add to the richness of the experience. I can already tell that this is going to be the refuge I need in this city. It's the place where I can come to work and unwind. "I did."

"I'll be outside waiting for you in twenty minutes."

I stare at my phone as the line goes dead.

***

"You don't like the salad?" He tilts his chin towards my plate before pushing another forkful of pasta into his mouth.

"It's fine." I run my index finger over the rim of the water glass sitting in front of me. "I'm not that hungry."

"You're thinking about what happened last night." He takes another bite of his food before washing it down with a swallow of the domestic beer he ordered. "I've been thinking about it too."

I look at him directly, astonished that he can fluidly move from talking about how warm it is outside today to diving into the finer details of our intimate encounter in his office. I had wanted to blurt out how much I enjoyed it the moment I stepped through the front doors of the library to see him sitting on one of the concrete steps wearing faded jeans and a blue dress shirt. He was as handsome as ever in the bright sunshine of this Saturday afternoon. My heart stalled when he turned towards me and a wide grin flashed across his lips.

"It's hard not to think about it," I say quietly not wanting the words to reveal the desperate desire that is fueling them.

His brow arches. "We should talk about it, Lilly. I need to clarify a few things with you."

My heart drops at the words. I've dated several men the last few years and whenever a discussion begins with a need for clarification it usually ends in a promise to stay friends. Clive is already regretting what happened between us and that's going to make it uncomfortable every time I have to discuss anything at work with him.

"I'm thirty-four years old." He pulls the linen napkin over his mouth before he tosses it onto his now empty plate. "I don't date women your age."

This is the rumor that Kathryn was talking about last night. "Women my age?"

"You're twenty-two." He taps his finger against the bottle of beer. "I have a hard limit about dating anyone your age. It's mostly about interests and life goals."

I suddenly feel all the lingering elation that I've been carrying with me since last night dissipating. "I'm too young for you?"

47

His hand leaps to his face to trace a path around his mouth. I stare at his long fingers remembering how it felt to come just by his touch. When I'd gotten back to the apartment, I'd crawled into my bed and had run my hands through my tender core to relive what it felt like when he expertly brought me to orgasm. Judging by the conversation we're having now, that one taste of pleasure with Clive Parker was all I was going to get.

"You're very young." He doesn't elaborate beyond that.

My eyes move past him to rest on a row of barstools that sit empty. Later this evening, the restaurant we're sitting in will shift to something else. The families and newly dating couples that now fill the cramped space will move on with their days. Men and women looking for something raw, primitive and fleeting will pour through the doors when the murky dusk takes over the city. They'll meet, they'll drink and then they'll retreat to a hotel down the street or maybe an apartment uptown where they'll fuck before they even know each other's names.

This is a city where casual sex is just around the corner and if I need that, I'll be able to find it without any trouble at all. I can replace my body's desire for Clive Parker with another gorgeous man. What I can't replace is my job.

"I completely understand." I cross my arms over my chest in a thoughtless gesture to protect my own emotions. I let myself feel too much when I came in his office last night. It's a mistake I'm not going to make again. I have to stay focused solely on my career. I can't let that slip through my fingers. "Let's just forget it ever happened."

"Forget it ever happened?" He rakes his hand through his tousled hair. "I don't want that."

The statement hits me with the brute force of a slap across the face. "What do you want then?"

"You." His hands fall to the table with a simultaneous heavy thud. "I want you, Lilly."

Chapter 13

I tangle my hands in his hair as he glides his lips over mine, deepening the lush kiss. I'm pressed against the door of my apartment, my back pushing against the wood, and his hard body rocking into me.

"Lilly." My name escapes his mouth and flutters over my lips. "Christ, Lilly."

We'd agreed after we finished our lunch that he'd bring me home and we'd meet this evening for dinner at his condo. Judging by how greedy his mouth is, I know that the promise of what awaits me later today will make every other intimate encounter I've had with a man pale in comparison. Clive has kissed me for the past fifteen minutes and the raw sexual energy that is flowing from his body into mine is unlike anything I've ever felt before. I can feel every ounce of desire within me pooling between my legs.

I pull my hands from his hair to reach behind me fumbling for the doorknob. I need to get inside. I need to come before I explode in a heated rush just from the taste of his mouth. I've never been this close to an orgasm without any direct stimulation. I know it's not going to take much to push me over the edge.

His hands are on mine before I have time to react pushing them over my head against the wood. "I can't get enough of you. I want to tie you to my bed and..."

I moan at the suggestion. It's what I want. The thought of him taking control of my body stalls my breathing. "I want that," I whisper against the softness of his beard.

His lips seal over mine again. His tongue pushes into my mouth, charting a path over the edge of my bottom lip before diving inside. He licks my tongue softly and tenderly before his teeth clamp down on my lip. The soft edge of pain pulls an uncontrollable moan from deep within me.

"We don't like behavior like this in the building." An older woman's voice yanks Clive's body instantly from mine.

My eyes jump past his shoulder to where one of the neighbors has poked her head out from the doorway of her apartment. "I'm…I'm sorry," I stammer vaguely aware of the pressure of his erection against me again.

"I should go inside," I whisper as I stare into his eyes. "I'll get ready for tonight."

"You'll touch yourself until you come." He leans forward as he growls the words softly into my ear." Don't do it, Lilly. You're going to save it for me."

I nod slowly knowing that even though my body is aching for release, I won't give in to the temptation. I want him to experience it with me. "I'll save it."

"I'll send a car for you at seven." His lips touch mine softly as he holds my face in his palms. "I can't wait."

* * *

"Your breasts are beautiful." His hand cups the heavy flesh as he traces his tongue quickly over the swollen bud of my right nipple. "I knew when I saw the picture that they'd be this soft and perfect."

I moan as I arch my back trying to steal even more sensation from his skilled tongue and lips. After I walked through the door of his apartment, he'd taken my hand and brought me to his bedroom. I hadn't resisted at all when he'd stripped all my clothing off and lowered me onto the bed.

"Look how hard your nipples are." He blows his breath across them. "They're aching for me, aren't they?"

"Yes," I whisper softly into the quiet peace of the room. It's a large space, decorated clearly with a man's taste in mind. My eyes had shot to the bed the moment he brought me into the room. The dark wooden headboard is imposing. The fact that it holds the promise of restraining me only adds to its allure.

His teeth clamp down tightly on my right nipple, the soft burst of pain racing straight to my core. I shift my legs uncontrollably trying to mask the pool of wetness that I can feel seeping from me.

"You're making me break all my rules, Lilly." He's hovering above me now. His gorgeous face sporting a wicked grin. He's wearing a navy blue t-shirt and jeans and even though it's a direct contrast to the expensive, tailored suits I usually see him dressed in,

50

the energy coming from him is the same. He's demanding, controlling and ready to take whatever he wants from me.

"What rules?" I ask to keep him in place. I want to stare at his face for a moment longer. I want to etch each fine line and nuance into my memory.

He pivots back on his heels, his hand jumping to the bottom of his t-shirt. He pulls it over his head in one swift movement. I stare at the muscular contours of his chest and stomach. His bicep bulges as he arches his arm so he can rake his hand through his hair. "I don't date women your age and I want to date you."

I smile as I reach up to graze my hand across the button of his jeans. I want him to be as naked and exposed as I am. "You're going to break that rule for me."

He pulls my hand into his quickly, yanking it from his waist. "I usually have a woman on her knees before I'll ever touch her body."

My eyes dart down to his crotch and the definable outline of his large erection through the fabric of his jeans. "I want to suck..."

"You will." His lips press into the palm of my hand after he brings it to his mouth. "You're going to slide that pretty mouth of yours over my cock. You're going to make me come all your beautiful face just like you said in the letter."

I push my cheek into the pillow. I'm suddenly awash with embarrassment. I'd forgotten about the letter I wrote to Parker. "I want to do it now."

"No." He leans forward again until the softness of his beard pushes against my cheek. "Tonight is for me. Tonight I get to have your beautiful body."

I moan softly as I feel his lips touch mine before he moves back, pulling his face across my flesh. My breath catches as I feel him push my legs apart with his shoulders. I cry out when his tongue slides softly over my cleft and I bury both my hands in his hair as he sucks my swollen clit between his lips.

"You're more beautiful here than I imagined." He licks incessantly at me; pulling everything I'm feeling right to the surface. "You're so ripe. You taste so good."

"Please, like that," I push the words from my lips. "Just like that."

"Like this," he whispers into my moist flesh. "Just like this."

I hold tightly to his hair as I grind my hips into his face. The groans falling from him into my core only spur me on more. I don't resist as he pushes my legs even farther apart. His tongue darts inside of me before he trails it back to my clit.

I feel the edge of the orgasm bearing down on me. "I'm so close."

He grunts as his tongue tightens its focus. I gyrate helplessly, my body's own natural needs taking over. Everything dims as I feel the overwhelming rush of the orgasm hit me with the force of a hurricane. I scream loudly, unable to curb what my body needs to express. He licks my lightly, softly and tenderly as I fall back from the edge.

I close my eyes when I feel the brush of his beard against my thigh. I listen intently as I hear the soft whisper of a zipper being pulled down and then the tear of a foil packet.

I whimper when I feel his legs between mine, forcing mine apart. His weight bears down on me. His strong hands grab mine, pushing them above my head. I take in a steely breath knowing that he's not going to be gentle. That moment has passed.

"Look at me, Lilly." His breath grazes my chin. "Look at me."

I open my eyes to see his handsome face above me. I try to look down to catch a glimpse of his cock but it's settled between my legs. I can feel how heavy and hard it is. "Kiss me," I say softly wanting to feel his mouth on mine as he takes me for the first time.

He acquiesces. His lush, full lips glide over mine just at the very moment he rams his thick, long cock into me in one fluid motion.

I bite his lip to quell my need to scream. He pulls back, his eyes showing the pleasure he took from the small burst of pain. "You feel so good, Lilly. So good."

His hips grind into me, each movement deeper than the last. I pull my legs around his waist wanting him to sink as far as he can within me.

I'm rewarded with a deep groan as he pumps harder and faster. "Fuck, yes, " he cries out between thrusts. "It's...so...good."

I struggle to free my hands, wanting to dig my nails into the soft curve of his ass as he takes me to the edge again. He doesn't let go of me. His head flies back as he ups the tempo, curse words flowing from his lips.

I clench around him as I climax in a heated rush, my legs falling onto the bed before they flail helplessly from the force of the pleasure. He pushes harder on my hands, drops his lips back to mine and calls my name into my mouth as his hips pump his own release.

Chapter 14

"Is this business or pleasure?" I ask before I step over the threshold and into his office.

"Both." He doesn't look up from where he's sitting behind his desk. "Please come in and close the door behind you."

I do as I'm told mainly because it's now Monday morning and after Clive had licked me to another orgasm at his condo on Saturday night, he'd taken me out for an expensive dinner before dropping me at home. I had spent the bulk of yesterday in bed, reliving the best sexual experience I'd ever had over-and-over again in my mind.

"You look lovely today." His eyes float over the plain black dress I'm wearing. "You look lovely every day."

I take the compliment with a smile. "I'm glad you think so."

"Sit, Lilly." He motions to the two leather chairs sitting in front of his desk. "I need to discuss something with you."

I feel a sense of loss being so near him, yet not having the ability to touch him. I haven't failed to notice that he hasn't gotten up from his seat to greet me. "Something about work?"

He swallows hard before he speaks, "I usually spend my time with women who are in the spotlight."

That's a kind way of saying he dates models and actresses. I'm still checking Google every morning to see if any new photographs of Clive and a new beautiful woman pop up. So far, since I've started working here, there's been nothing to add to the bounty of images already out there. I shouldn't be as grateful for that as I am, but I can't help it. After the tender moments I spent with him in his bed two nights ago, I want him all to myself.

"I've never dated someone like you." He tips his chin in my direction. "You're very different."

"Different?" I parrot back because right now I don't know whether to absorb that as a good thing or a bad thing.

"Most of my relationships…," he stalls closing his eyes briefly. "Most of the women I've been involved with haven't been interested in what I do for a living. Their focus tends to be directed towards other things."

"I understand," I offer to keep him talking. I want to understand although I don't really right at this moment.

"You're the smartest woman I've ever met," he says the words without any hesitation at all. "I knew it the moment you laced into me about how the dating app was a piece of shit."

I smile at the reminder of that day. I'd taken the bold stance of telling it like it was with the hope that I'd be able to secure a position in his organization. I never imagined it would land me a spot in his bed, under his beautiful body, too.

"I don't know where this is going." His hand flies into the air between us. "It's fun to be around you."

I was hoping for more and if he asked me, I'd tell him that fun doesn't even begin to describe the range of emotions I feel whenever I'm in the same room with him. I respect him as a businessman and I desire him as a lover. "I like being around you too, Clive."

"I need to say this and please, Lilly, please don't misinterpret it." He pushes his hands against his desk, pulling himself to his feet. I watch in silence as he rounds his desk until he stops right in front of me.

"I won't." I try to sound genuine even though I'm bracing myself for the worst.

"I want us to spend as much time together outside the office as we can. I need that. It's just that…" his voice trails.

"You need for us to stay professional here at the office?" I ask hoping that he'll confirm my suspicions.

"For your sake, yes." He crosses his legs at the ankle, leaning back into the edge of his desk. "I don't want your co-workers treating you differently because we're sleeping together."

"I can be completely professional." I nod my head to reiterate the point. "Is that all?"

"No." His hands clench the edge of his desk. "There's something else."

"What?" I try to level my voice.

His right hand darts towards me. "Come here."

I stand quickly, pushing my hand into his. I don't hesitate as he pulls his arms around my waist so I'm resting against his chest.

"I'm not close to many people," he whispers into my hair. "Most of the people I've loved in my life are now gone."

I know that he's referring to his family. The magazine and newspaper articles I've read about him have detailed how his family fell apart after Coral died. I understand completely the need to shelter's one heart after it suffers a devastating loss. "I'm sorry you've lost so much."

"I'll tell you more about it soon, Lilly. I need to."

I'm counting on it. It's the opening I need to share my past with him.

Chapter 15

"Christ, Lilly." His hands are tangled in my hair, pulling at it harshly. "It's the middle of the morning."

I don't care. When he'd held me in his arms moments ago I felt a desperate need to give him the same pleasure he gave to me the other night. I've craved the taste of his big, beautiful cock since I saw him walk into Star Bistro. Now, I'm on my knees, his pants hung open and the thick root pushing between my lips.

"I knew you'd suck my cock like this," he hisses the words into the still air. "Harder, Lilly, harder."

I pull as much of it as I can into my mouth, pivoting back on my heels to give me more leverage. I grip tightly to the base with my left hand as the right moves to cup his heavy, full balls.

The words he's trying to say morph into something primal and guttural. His hips bounce against the hard edge of his desk as he rocks himself into me. I murmur around the thickness, relishing in the feeling of the lush head as my tongue runs around it over and over again.

"Yes, fuck." His hand moves to my neck and I flinch for just a moment before I find my rhythm again. I pump him hard and fast, my mouth opening wider to take as much of him as I can.

I pull back, popping the head out with a loud sound before I race my tongue over the plush crest. "I want you to come all over my face."

His cock jerks in my hands the moment the words leave my mouth. "Fuck, yes."

I pull the tip back between my moist lips, teasing and tempting it. I feel his balls constrict in my hand and I know he's nearing his release. A small burst of his pleasure spears onto my tongue and I pull back in that instant.

"I'm coming." His hand grips tightly on my neck, leveling my face at his crotch. His large hand circles the root as he pumps one endless stream after another onto my face and between my lips.

***

"I don't know how I'm supposed to function after that." He wipes the edge of my mouth with the pad of his thumb before he darts it between my lips. "I've never come that hard before."

It was so much that I'd struggled after pulling it into my mouth. The taste of him is strong and intoxicating. I'm aroused but I know that his day is filled with meetings and planning and mine is filled with working on the improvements to the dating app.

"I need to go to Orlando for a few days." He kisses the top of my forehead. "I should have planned to bring you with me."

"That would raise suspicion." I step back as he refastens his pants and belt. "Everyone would be talking about that."

"You're one of the best developers we have." He runs his finger across my jaw. "You're actually the best. It would make sense for you to start sitting in on some meetings and traveling with me."

I can't shield the glint of excitement in my eye. "You would let me do that?"

"I want you to do that." His hand glides from my chin to my neck. "We'll discuss it further when I'm back."

I nod in agreement. I know that my ideas can help his business and I'm grateful that he's recognizing it. I can't tell if that's tied in to his desire to be near me but I know that he's ruthless when it comes to protecting his business interests. He trusts me. I hear it in his words, but more than that I see it in his face.

"Lilly?" He tilts his chin down to catch my gaze. "Were you in an accident?"

My eyes dart over his face trying to mask the panic I suddenly feel wash over me. "An accident?"

He runs his index finger over a jagged, circular scar on the back of my neck. "I just noticed this when you were on your knees. It's a scar, isn't it?"

I reach back to try and move his hand but it's immobile. I cover his with my own. "It's a scar, yes."

"How did you get that?"

"It happened at home a few years ago." I shake my head trying to find a reasonable explanation but in my anguished state I draw a blank. "I'm fine now."

"You're more than fine." He takes the bait, pulling his arms around me. "Judging by what happened here today, you're incredible."

Chapter 16

"Lilly, we'd like you to come up with a list of suggestions regarding our security system." Clive's head-of-security, Jordan, doesn't look up from her tablet. "They don't have to be detailed, but if you'd take some time to go over what we have in place now, we'd appreciate it."

"Do you have time to come in tomorrow to assess things, Lilly?" Clive finally looks at me. "It won't take more than a few hours."

I shouldn't feel as despondent over this meeting as I do. When Clive's assistant, Bruce, had called me to ask me to come to his office I was giddy. His business trip finally ended last night and even though we'd shared dozens of text messages and several calls since he left four days ago, I'm craving the taste of his mouth and the feeling of his body. I wanted to meet him at the airport when his flight landed two hours ago but I know that asking for that privilege would make me look desperate. Instead, I focused on my work until the call to come here. The moment I walked into the office and saw Jordan sitting next to Clive, my heart sank.

"Of course," I tap my heel against the floor. "Is there anything in particular you're concerned about regarding security?"

"A set of fresh eyes is always a good thing." Clive stands and shoves his hands into the pockets of his pants. "If you can give us a time now, Jordan will arrange to be here."

Her head shoots up and she throws him a glance that screams *'fuck you'*. "What time works for you?"

I know the question is directed at me, even though the sarcasm dripping from it is aimed at Clive. "I can be here by ten. Does that work for you?"

"I can do that." She's on her feet quickly, not acknowledging me at all. "Check in at the security desk in the lobby and then come up here."

I nod, realizing that I can't say anything that will alter her mood. She's just as pissed as I am that this work week has just been extended with little notice.

"I'll see you out." Clive reaches to grab Jordan's elbow.

I take that as a cue for me to leave too, so I pull myself up from the chair. "I'll do my best to offer some useful suggestions, Mr. Parker."

"You'll wait here for me, Lilly." He motions towards the couch. "I'll be back."

I try to contain the grin that is forcing itself onto my lips. "I'll be right here."

***

"If my day wasn't so busy I'd fuck you right here, right now." His lips push into mine again; gliding over them with the same heated rush I feel building within me.

"You can fuck me tonight," I offer out of the unreserved need that is a constant presence inside of me. I've been craving his body since he left for his trip days ago.   We've only been intimate a few times, but they've burned a place in my mind that can't be filled with anything else. I find myself jumping back to the erotic touch of his tongue on my core when I'm trying to work and it's impossible for me to fall asleep without coming while thinking about his cock inside of me.

"I need to go to Boston tonight to see my nephew." He rests his forehead against mine. "He's under the weather. I got him some books and toys in Orlando to cheer him up."

He's never mentioned anyone in his family other than Parker, but I know about Cory. I know that he's the biological son of Clive's sister, Christina. "Is it serious?"

"No." He pulls me closer by wrapping both of his hands around my shoulders. "It's something he picked up at school. He'll be fine in a few days. He just needs rest."

I nuzzle my cheek into his chest, soaking in the natural fragrance of him combined with the delicious cologne he uses. "Will you call me when you're back?"

"The minute I'm back in New York, I'll call."

Chapter 17

"Clive is going to appreciate every one of these suggestions, Lilly." Jordan gestures towards a row of chilled water bottles sitting on a counter near her desk. "Do you want more water?"

I shake my head with a small giggle. "I've had three. I think I've had my limit for the day."

She laughs heartily as she places the almost empty bottle that is in her hand down before picking up another. "I can do with one more. After that, cut me off."

I smile back at her, glad that we've hit it off as well as we have. After I arrived and we dove into the framework of the security system currently in place at Corteck, she'd taken a call from her four-year-old son. She put him on speaker phone so he could say hello to me and my heart had flipped at the sound of such a precious, young voice. It brought to the surface a rush of emotions I wouldn't be able to explain away so I'd excused myself to use the restroom while she finished talking to him.

"You should come over for dinner one night." She runs her hand over my forearm as she settles back into the chair next to me at her desk. "Do you have a boyfriend? You can bring him too."

"I don't have a boyfriend." I try not to laugh too heartily. I don't want to give anything away. Technically, Clive isn't my boyfriend so I'm not lying. "I just got to New York. I've been too busy with work to go out."

"My husband has a lot of single friends." She twists the plastic cap back onto the bottle of water she's still holding in her hands. "We can invite someone over for dinner when you come."

I scratch my neck while I stare at her face. The wide grin that covers her mouth is addictive. I can't help but smile back at her. "I'm not sure I'm ready to date yet. I'm still trying to find my feet."

"It's not a date." She turns back towards one of the two computer monitors we've been staring at for the past three hours. "You'll come for dinner. A handsome, available friend of my husband's will come for dinner and we'll eat. It's simple."

Life is never that simple. My life stopped being simple when Clive Parker slid his fingers into my panties.

"I do want to make new friends in the city." I cock a brow. "I don't see how it can hurt."

"Perfect." She slides her chair closer to me. "We'll do it on Tuesday."

"Tuesday it is."

***

It's Tuesday. For most people that means they're inching closer to the weekend. For me, it means another day that has passed since Clive spoke to me. I've been telling myself that I haven't heard anything from him because the man runs a corporation that employs more than a thousand people worldwide. I've also been convincing myself that what is happening between us is simple and uncomplicated and I need to keep it that way.   He said he'd call and I have to trust in that even though I called Bruce yesterday and found out Clive was in his office all day with the door shut. I sent him a few text messages asking how his nephew was doing. I finally called him last night and left a voicemail but the only response has been empty silence.

I need to focus on my work and on picking up a bouquet of flowers to take over to Jordan's house for dinner tonight. Judging by the fact that Clive is intentionally avoiding me, meeting a new man might be the best thing for my bruised ego. I've been dumped enough times to know when it's within distance, staring at me like a neon sign on the horizon.

"Lilly?" Dan's voice shakes me from my thoughts as he rounds the corner and suddenly appears in front of my desk. "I'm here to give you a heads-up."

"A heads-up?" I parrot back. "About what?"

"Mr. Parker." He doesn't continue beyond that even though I'm staring at him with my mouth hanging open.

"What about him?" I push back.

"Lilly." I hear Clive's voice before I see his tall frame. He walks with the confidence of a man on a mission. Apparently, right now, that mission involves me. "We need to talk."

"I'm listening." I don't look up from my computer's screen to acknowledge his presence. "What is it, Mr. Parker?"

He rests his hand on the edge of my monitor and I'm fearful for just a moment that the weight of his body will cause it to snap in half. "I'd like you to come with me to my office."

"Right now?" I adjust my hands slightly, pulling them into my lap.

"Right now, Lilly." He turns quickly on his heel as he heads back down the corridor towards the bank of elevators.

"What the hell is going on?" Dan can't hide his curiosity. It's literally seeping out from each of the words. "Do you have any idea what that's about?"

"I don't," I lie. "I have no idea at all."

Chapter 18

"I expected you to be right behind me, Lilly." He reaches past me to push his office door closed with a loud thud. "I held the elevator for more than four minutes waiting for you."

I've held my breath for the past four days waiting for him so I'd say we're even.

"I had to save what I've been working on." That's the second lie I've told in the last ten minutes although this time there's a ribbon of truth in it. I'd been working on something all morning and the idea of walking away from my desk without backing it up was terrifying to me.

He studies my face briefly as if he's weighing the merit of my words. "You're a conscientious worker. I'll give you that."

It's exactly the words any woman wants to hear when she's blindly attracted to a man. How utterly unromantic of you, Mr. Parker.

"I think I know why you've called me here," I say it calmly. We moved beyond the expected protocol of me playing the naïve, new employee when I came in a heated rush while pressed up against the window. It's the same window that I can't bring myself to look at right now.

"Really?" He slides his suit jacket off before he removes one silver cuff link, followed by the other.

If we're getting comfortable, I might as well join in. I pull off the black blazer I've been wearing all day over my yellow sundress. "Yes."

I watch in silence as he pushes the sleeves of his dress shirt over his elbows, revealing his muscular forearms. "I doubt that you know why I called you into my office, Lilly."

A fleeting image of him pulling me over his knee and giving my ass a quick spank floats through my mind. I shake my head to chase it away. "You're having second thoughts about us, aren't you?"

"Us?" he asks with enough sincerity in his tone that I can sense it's genuine.

"Yes." I cross my arms over my chest. "You called me in here to talk about that."

He cocks a brow before he walks over to a cabinet near his desk. I don't move as I watch him pour himself a half glass of bourbon. He downs it quickly and effortlessly in one gulp. Considering it's barely past noon, I'd venture a safe guess that talking about what happened between us is more difficult for him than I imagined it would be.

"We can chalk it up to a stupid decision." I don't want my voice to crack as much as it does when I say the words. "We don't have to talk about it again. I just don't want to lose my job."

He pivots quickly on his heel until he's facing me directly. "Your job?"

"I need this job." I drop my hands to my side. "I don't want to lose it."

He steps towards me. "You should have thought about that before you did it."

I recoil physically from the words, stumbling backwards. "I'm going to lose my job because of what we did?"

He stops mid-step to stare at me his hand flying wildly in the air. "You think you're going to lose your job because we fucked?"

I rest my forehead against my fingers trying to find a way to salvage the only job that's ever held any meaning for me. "I can't change what happened, Mr. Parker… Clive," I pause. "I know you think I'm the kind of woman who just jumps into bed with anyone. I don't blame you for thinking that after you saw that picture and read that letter, but…I'm not like that."

"Stop." His hand darts into the air between us. "Just stop."

I clamp my left hand over my mouth for good measure. My natural inclination is to fight tooth and nail to hold onto this. It's how I've lived my life up to this point. Standing idly by while something this important is taken away from me is taking every ounce of strength I have.

"You crossed a line." He takes a heavy, determined step towards me.

"What line?" I say into a small breath. "I have no idea what line."

"I know about your latest personal project, Lilly." He reaches to grab my arm. "I know that you're developing an organ donation app. You think you can use what happened to my sister to further your career."

"What?" I bark the word out as I try to take a step back. "How do you know about that?"

His eyes scan my face, stopping to drink in the confusion that has to be clouding my expression. "Who do you think you are? You can't just waltz into my life and use the death of someone I love to make a few dollars."

The words bite through me so ferociously that I feel a physical ache within my chest. "You don't know what you're talking about."

"I know exactly what I'm talking about." His hand finally drops from me. "You got the idea for the app when Parker told you about Coral, didn't you?"

"Parker never told me about Coral." The words are sincere. Parker's sole focus during our exchanges had been finding a way into my bed.

"I'll ask him right now." He takes a few long strides towards his desk. "I can call him this minute."

"Go ahead." I move back until I feel the welcome oasis of the couch pressed against the back of my knees. I lower myself onto it.

I watch as he dials a number. He waits patiently before slamming the phone back into its receiver. "He didn't answer."

I don't respond because I have absolutely nothing to say to him. I'm stunned that he's accusing me of trying to garner some sort of financial gain by using the fact that his sister's organs were harvested after her death in a car accident. My relentless need to create the app has nothing to do with him at all. I should tell him that but my curiosity about how he knows about its existence is too overwhelming to ignore.

"How do you know about the app?" I look directly at him. "Tell me how you know."

Chapter 19

He leans against the desk, his voice a harsh whisper. "Your employment contract gives me unlimited access to any computer you own."

My gaze narrows as I feel a dull pit forming in my stomach. "I have the files for the app on my laptop. I've never brought it to the office."

His jaw tightens. "I was visiting Rebecca on Saturday while you were here with Jordan. I accessed the files then."

My eyes close as I take in a deep breath. It's why he wanted me to live with her. He hasn't trusted my motives since he walked into Star Bistro weeks ago. I shudder as I think about all the information I've stored on my laptop. I feel exposed in a way I've never before.

"I saw the schematics for the app. It's brilliant. You want to give donor families the chance to connect with the recipients of the harvested organs. I found the framework and I read your testing files," he spits the words out violently at me. "You even used the control sequence of a teenage woman as the donor. I thought you were smarter than that."

I push my head back as I let out a single, solitary breath. "You ordered me down here to go over your security files so you could violate me."

"Violate you?" He doesn't even try to suppress the chuckle that escapes his lips. "I had a right to see those files. I knew you weren't being honest with me. I had Bruce run a background check on you yesterday. You didn't exist until you enrolled in MIT."

The actions sting more than his words. After the intimacy we've shared and the promises he's made to me, the fact that he still doesn't trust me rips through me with the force of a jagged knife. "I can't believe you went behind my back to rummage through my personal computer."

His hands jump to his hips. "I can't believe you'd use someone else's pain to make a profit."

"That's not what I'm doing." I push my hand against the arm of the couch to find the strength to pull myself up. I have absolutely no faith that my legs will support me right now. "You have no idea what you're talking about."

"The information on your computer is cut and dry." He clenches his right hand into a fist and slams it against the edge of his desk. "I saw what you're doing with my own two eyes. You haven't been truthful with me. You wanted a position here so you can use my contacts to launch your app and you wanted my sister's name attached to it for all the sympathy it's going to bring."

It's a concept that might have some merit if my own past wasn't more tragic than his. "That's honestly how you see me? You think I'm capable of that?"

"I don't think you're capable of it." His hand leaps to my chin. "I know you are. I saw the proof myself."

I push against his chest to free myself of his touch. The same hand that falls from my face is the one that stroked my cheek and brought me pleasure. So much has changed so quickly. "I quit."

"If you think you're walking away with those files, you're going to have a fight on your hands, Lilly Randall," he hisses the words at me. "I'm going to sue you."

"It's not Randall." I look directly into his eyes. "My name isn't Lilly Randall."

"What?"

"It's Lilly Vanderwelle." I yank my jacket into my hand before I brush past him to move towards the door of his office.

"Wait." He reaches for my arm but I'm beyond his grasp. "I've heard that name before."

"I'm not surprised." I turn as I twist the door handle in my palm.

"In the paper." His eyes are instantly alert and locked on my face. "On the news. I remember the name was everywhere."

"Yes, everywhere," I repeat back. It had been everywhere. Every major newspaper in the country had splashed the headline across their front page.

His expression is impassive as he pushes for more. "What was it? Goddammit, you tell me what the fuck is going on. Why are you using a fake name to work here?"

I cast my gaze down trying to find a way to calm my overwrought emotions. "It's actually very simple, Mr. Parker."

"Tell me." His hand waves in the air as if to spur me on.

I spit out the words one-by-one trying to detach myself from them. "Six years ago my father came home from a graveyard shift at the factory he worked at. He walked into the room my two younger brothers shared and shot them both at point blank range. Then he came into the room I was in with my older sister. He shot her before he turned the gun on me." I rub my hand over the scar on the back of my neck, closing my eyes as I recall the sounds and smells of that moment. "My mother was last before he pushed the gun into his throat and pulled the trigger."

"Christ, Lilly." His voice cracks but I can't bring myself to look at his face.

"I was the only survivor." I bite my lip to try and ward off the onslaught of tears that always rips through me when I think of my family. "My mother's heart is inside a stranger's body. My four-year-old brother's liver saved a young woman's life. My sister's cornea gave someone their sight back and everyone I've ever loved is gone."

I don't hear anything he's saying as I pull open the door, walk through and don't look back.

GONE

Part Two

Chapter 1

"I told someone." I don't elaborate as I stare past his shoulder towards a group of women who have settled into the chairs at a table next to us.

The toe of his shoe pushes against mine when he slides it across the tiled floor. "Someone you work with or a friend?"

I wouldn't define Clive Parker as my friend. I feel a small smile fleetingly drift over my lips at the notion that we would ever be friends. I worked for him. We had sex. I don't know how to explain that so I won't. "He owns the company I worked at."

"Worked at?" He leans forward until his elbows catch the edge of the small, circular table. "What does that mean?"

Avoiding eye contact with him isn't going to change the scope of this conversation. I came to the hospital to talk to him. He's the only person I can confide in and if I want to leave this cafeteria feeling less emotionally spent than I do, I have to be honest with him. "I quit my new job, Ben."

"Lil." He straightens in his chair. "When we were texting last week you told me you landed a job at Corteck."

It's a statement. It's not a question but the implied expectation of a response is there. "I'm talking about Corteck. That's the job I quit."

"All you've talked about for the past few years is working there." He raises one dark brow as his brown eyes scan my face. "You're telling me you finally got a job there and then quit after telling the owner about..."

The words drift off the same way they usually do when the conversation turns towards the topic of my family. It's been this way since I met Ben Foster in the grief support group I sought solace in after I was shot. He's a doctor, but more than that, he's become an older brother to me. I see the same pain I feel within me when I look in his eyes. His mother died when he was a teenager so he understands my loss in ways most people can't.

"Why did you tell him?" He taps his index finger over the top of my hand. "More importantly, why did you quit after telling him?"

I pull my hand away to run it over the length of my hair, smoothing it as I do. "He accused me of something and I told him about my past to prove that he was wrong."

I see the hesitation in his expression before he speaks. "What did he accuse you of?"

I knew that there was a strong possibility when I came to see Ben that he'd ask me that question. I haven't shared the painful details of what happened in Clive's office before I quit my job with anyone. After bolting out of Corteck's headquarters, I went straight to the apartment I shared with Rebecca. I'd thrown everything I owned back into the two suitcases I brought with me to New York and I raced out of the building even though it was the middle of the day and she was still at work. She'd tried to call and text me several times since I moved out two days ago, but I have nothing to say to her. She's Clive's friend and she had to have known that he wanted me to live with her so he could hunt through my computer when I wasn't home.

"Do you remember that app that I talked about?" I know I can move the conversation in a different direction but I came here to lean on his strong, broad shoulders and I have to open up if that's going to happen.

"The one I helped you with?" His face brightens instantly. "I've been thinking more about it. I think there's a way we can improve it."

I smile at his reference to the medical travel app that he helped me develop. When I had initially brought up the idea with him, he'd jumped at the chance to participate. Given his expertise as an emergency room physician, it only made sense that I took his input and ran with it. "I want to hear about that. I have a check for your percentage of sales from last month."

"I told you that I don't want any of that." He smiles. "You did all the work to get it out there. All I did was offered some advice."

He's being modest. It's a character trait of Ben's that I've long admired. He does good work in the world and rarely takes any credit for it. His latest focus has been a new charitable endeavor that helps individuals who don't have the financial means to get the medical care they need. He's partnered with his fiancée, Kayla, to launch the Foster Foundation. It's a non-profit in memory of his mother that he's working on alongside his twin brother, Noah. Each and every time he tells me about it I feel an unwelcome bite of envy. He has a family and they are working together to make a difference in people's lives. It's what I'm trying to do with the organ donor app.

"I'd like to donate your percentage to the Foundation if you won't take it," I say it while trying to hold in my emotion. I know how much Ben wants to help others and if I can contribute to that, as a silent way to thank him for always being there for me, it's something I feel compelled to do.

"I'd like that." He nods slowly. "Let's get back to Corteck. Tell me what happened, Lil."

"I had to sign some contracts before I started working there." I scrub my hand across my face. "One of them gave my boss access to any computer I own."

"What?" His brow furrows. "How can they do that? It seems like an invasion of privacy to me."

Defending Clive Parker's employment requirements isn't on my to-do list today but I'm the one who signed the form without thoroughly reading it. "I think it's a standard thing when you work for a tech firm. They're all protective of their future developments."

"So someone went through your work computer?" He tilts his chin towards me. "What did they find? You were surfing on gossip sites when you should have been working?"

I'm not a gossip hound but I find it amusing that Ben's pegged me as one. I wish the issue were something as simple and innocent as that. "It was my personal laptop. All of my files about the organ donor app I've been working on are on there."

He leans back in the plastic chair he's sitting in as he studies my face. "Shit, Lil. That must have pissed you off. I know how protective you are about that."

He knows that because each time I've brought up the app with him, I've asked him to keep it between us. As much as I feel it will benefit anyone involved in an organ donation, it's also an emotionally wrenching subject for me. If I'm being completely honest with myself, I'm not even sure I'll ever have the fortitude to bring the app to market. If I do, I want it to be available free of charge. Making a profit off of anyone involved in such a difficult situation isn't appealing to me at all.

"That's why you quit, isn't it?" He pushes the question out between clenched teeth and before I have a chance to respond, he continues, "I can go down there and give them a piece of my mind if you want."

I grin across the table at him. This is the part of him that I need and cherish. Ben is the closest thing I have to a family now since my grandmother died just over a year ago. "You don't need to be a superhero," I joke. "I can take care of myself."

He playfully raises his arm, flexing his right bicep beneath the fabric of his white lab coat. "I know you can but while we're on that topic, what are you doing for work now?"

Even though the notion of going back to Boston to work at the café has crossed my mind more than a dozen times, I won't do it. I'm in New York City and since my dream job is now over and done with, I'm moving on to bigger, and hopefully, better things. "I've started applying at some other tech firms."

He scratches his neck while he studies my face. "I have a solution in the interim."

"What?" I ask with a wide smile on my face. Ben's solutions to life's problems almost always involve him opening his wallet. He's generous to a fault and I'm prepared to hear him offer me some money disguised as a loan he won't expect me to pay back.

"Kayla's been looking for someone to help her with some computer stuff with the Foundation." He takes a small sip of the coffee that's been sitting in the paper cup in front of him for the past twenty minutes. "Would you have time to go down to the office this week and give her a hand?"

Even if my schedule didn't consist of more than dropping off resumes and watching the television in my hotel room, I'd jump at the chance to help Ben. "I'll do it."

"Kayla can put you on contract for the time being." He pushes his hand against the table's edge, readying himself to stand. "I don't want your roommate tossing you out because you can't make rent."

This is where I tell him that I'm living in an extended stay hotel near LaGuardia airport. It's also the point where I ask him to help me with the one task I've been putting off for the past six years. "Ben, I wanted to talk about something else."

He stands just as the words leave my lips. "Can we talk later, Lil? I'm late to get back to the ER."

I nod with a faint smile as I feel his lips brush over my forehead before he turns and walks away.

Chapter 2

"Lilly."

I flinch when I hear his voice in the space behind me. It's not as though I can jump up from the chair I'm in and sprint across the crowded library towards the exit. I need to turn around and face him. That or I need to ignore him completely with the hope that he'll take the hint and leave me alone. I'm not one for subtle trickery though. I need to get this over with and the library, with its expected rules of protocol in place, seems like as good a spot as any.

"Mr. Parker." I twist around to look up at him. He's dressed in a tailored black suit and matching shirt. It's a stark and stunning look for mid-morning on a Friday.

"I'd like to speak to you." His eyes dart around the large room as if he's searching for a secluded corner that he can pull me into.

I motion with my hand to a chair next to where I'm sitting at a long, rectangular table. "We can talk here."

He hesitates before lowering himself into the wooden chair. The weight of his body pulls an audible creak from the weathered timber. "I'd prefer if we do this in private."

I don't look at him as I slowly close my laptop. My first instinct when I heard his voice was to slam it shut but I hadn't. He has already seen all the secrets I keep harbored on the hard drive so the need to shield it from his eyes seems illogical. It's much like a lover hiding behind the veil of a bed sheet after making love with the lights on.

"I prefer if we do it here." I slip my computer into the leather laptop bag I bought when I first started classes at MIT. It's worn and battered, but the familiarity it offers me is comforting in an abstract way.

"I've been looking for you since you walked out of my office."

I'm tempted to toss back a retort about wondering why he didn't just resort to the GPS tracking software that he installed on my computer when he helped himself to its contents a few days ago. I refrain though because it if I spit the words out he may see the sliver of truth that's woven into them. I had run several spyware programs on my laptop after I'd checked into the hotel but I found nothing at all. I don't trust him and I doubt that I need to announce that to him. "How did you know I'd be here?"

His gaze flies over the two people sitting near the end of the table. "I've been here six times the past three days. I hoped eventually you'd show up."

Predictability isn't a good bedfellow when you're trying to avoid someone you shouldn't have slept with in the first place. I came back to the library because I feel safe and understood here. Maybe it's the rows of books or perhaps it's just the expectation that you don't have to make small talk with anyone while you're here. I'm drawn to it because it reminds me of a time when I was a child and the world didn't feel as bitter and unfair as it does to me now.

"I haven't been answering your calls." I lean back to cross my legs, smoothing my hands over the fabric of my navy blue dress. "You should have taken the hint. Hunting me down was a waste of your time."

He mirrors my stance. His shoe taps against the leg of my chair as he crosses his own legs. "If I was hunting you down, Lilly, I would have found you immediately."

I don't doubt that. Even if he hadn't placed anything on my computer to track my whereabouts, he had the resources to find me in an instant. I had used the name Lilly Randall to check into the hotel. It's my legal name now although it still feels foreign whenever I introduce myself. It had been my mother's maiden name and each time I say or write it, I'm reminded of her gentle guidance. "What do you want?"

He studies my face before he answers, "I want to apologize."

I exhale softly. I should ask him what the apology is for. I want him to feel some sense of guilt over the fact that he was tender and loving in bed and then with calculated determination he made a conscious decision to pull me away from my home so he could gain access to my private files. I want him to feel badly about it but the growing knot in the pit of my stomach is telling me that he's not feeling anything but a sense of accomplishment.

"I didn't handle things very well." He pauses, "I had no idea about your family."

Talking about what happened won't change the facts of that day. All of the therapy sessions I've gone to and the grief support group meetings I've attended have taught me that. I've learned how to cope. Getting through each day now is less of a struggle than it was five years ago, but it will never be a subject I openly embrace. "I regret bringing it up."

"I pushed you into a corner," he says evenly. "I'm very protective of my sister's memory. When I saw those files on your computer I just assumed that you…"

"You just assumed that I was going to use her name to try and make a profit," I interrupt. "I get it."

He glances at me. "There's no way I could have known about your past, Lilly. If I had, I wouldn't have jumped on you the way I did."

"Mr. Parker." I uncross my legs, taking a moment to adjust the hem of my dress. "You made assumptions about me. I made assumptions about you. We were both wrong. I don't think we need to discuss this any further."

"What assumptions did you make about me?" His hand reaches to touch my thigh.

As tempted as I am to swat it away in a dramatic gesture of forbiddance, I don't. Drawing any attention to the two of us isn't my goal. I want to end this conversation so I have time to pull my emotions together before I go to the interview I have scheduled in a little over an hour. "I assumed that the man you were in bed was the same man you were in the office."

I watch his face, seeing the internal debate raging within. "I am the same man, Lilly."

"You once said I was too young." I reach to pull my laptop bag onto my legs. "I wanted to argue that point with you but I think you're right."

The only response he offers is a cock of his brow as he crosses his arms over his chest.

"I'm smart enough to know that I'm not mature enough to separate my feelings from sex." I hold his gaze as I continue, "I thought you trusted me after we made love. I guess I thought it meant something to you because it meant something to me."

"It did mean something to me." He exhales in a rush. "That's why it tore me up inside when I saw the files for the app on your computer. I thought you'd gone behind my back to develop something very personal to me."

I push myself to my feet, needing to gain distance from not only him, but also all of the emotions I've been keeping at bay for the past few days. "I understand why you'd think that. I know all about protecting the memory of the people we love. What I can't understand is that you felt the need to look at my computer at all. I guess I just thought that what happened between us…what happened at your place meant more than it did."

"It meant a lot to me." He stands. "I was only trying to protect myself. My business is the only thing I have left."

I bite my lip to fight off the urge to laugh in his face. "Your business is safe from me, Clive. I don't want anything to do with it or you."

"Don't say that, Lilly." He sighs. "This is all a big misunderstanding. I want to talk about you coming back to work. I want to talk about your family."

"No." I swallow past the sudden lump in my throat. "You must have dug up every detail you could about my family after I quit. I doubt there are any blanks I need to fill in for you."

The slight blush that rushes over his cheeks is all the confirmation I need. "I was concerned. You didn't expect me to ignore it, did you?"

Of course I didn't. Anyone in his position would have scrambled to find out as much as they could about that night six years ago. You can call it morbid fascination or genuine concern. Regardless, the results are the same. He researched what happened and he knows all the unforgiving facts about the one night that completely altered my life. I feel more exposed right now than I did three days ago when he accused me of being heartless all in pursuit of a dollar.

"I have to be somewhere." I glance over his shoulder to where a large, ornate clock is hanging on the wall. "We don't have anything left to discuss."

He shifts slightly on his feet as if he's clearing a path so I can move past him. "We're not done. I'll be in touch."

I don't acknowledge the comment. We are done. We were done the moment he opened my laptop, pressed the power button and broke my trust.

Chapter 3

"Did you nail that interview you had on Friday?" Ben looks up at me over the wine glass perched in his hand. "You went in there and wowed them, didn't you?"

I wish I could say that I had. The interview was at Hughes Enterprises for a junior programmer. I'd spent most of the hour correcting the woman interviewing me about the logistics of the position. It was obvious from the moment I walked into the office that she had no idea exactly what a programmer's job entails. I had schooled her on the finer points of technology all in a bid to convince myself that I deserved the low paying, entry level job she was offering me. As soon as I got back to my room at the hotel I scolded myself internally for sabotaging my chance at a job that would have at least got my foot in the door of a conglomerate that handles programming for some of the biggest firms in Europe.

"I blew it," I confess. I don't see any point in trying to dress up the utter disaster I'd made of my life. "I don't think I'll get the job."

"You're just being hard on yourself, Lil." He motions towards the waiter who has been hovering near us for the better part of the past ten minutes. "You're ready to order, right?"

I'm not hungry but given the fact that Ben made a reservation at one of the nicest restaurants in all of Manhattan to celebrate the success of our medical travel app, I can't offend him by asking if I can just munch away on the breadsticks while he eats. "I'll have whatever you're having."

"You must be starving," he shoots back. "I'm having a steak."

I roll my eyes. "I can handle a steak."

"You can handle anything, Lil," he begins before he stops to quickly order our entrees.

I wait until the waiter is out of earshot before I move my chair closer to the table. I've only heard about Axel NY and its sister location in Boston. I've never dined at either restaurant because the cost of this meal alone would cover my grocery bill for almost a month. "You didn't have to bring me to such a nice place, Ben."

The corner of his lip pops up into a bright smile. "I'm a doctor. I can afford it."

I laugh at the words. "Maybe when I get settled into a new apartment I can cook something for you and Kayla."

His expression freezes as his eyes flash across my face. "What do you mean? You're settling into a new apartment now, aren't you?"

Ben and I made a pact years ago that we wouldn't lie to one another. It had stemmed out of the desperate need we both felt to find someone we could trust implicitly. I don't know all the details of his life and he doesn't know everything that occurs in mine, but there's an unspoken understanding between the two of us that what we do share will always be based in truth.

"I moved out of that apartment." I take a small bite from one of the crunchy breadsticks that's been sitting in the basket the waiter brought for us along with our appetizer salads. "My roommate and I didn't hit it off."

He scratches his chin. "What did she do?"

"Maybe I did something," I say with a stunted chuckle.

"Did you leave wet towels on the floor?"

I hadn't. Rebecca had but it would never have been enough of a reason for me to pack up my belongings and give up my room. "She knows the owner of Corteck. They're close friends so it would have been too awkward for me to keep hanging out there."

"Where are you living now?" he presses.

Grateful for the end of the questioning about why I suddenly needed to change addresses, I try and put a positive spin on the dismal state of my living conditions. "I took a room at a long stay hotel. It's cheap and comfortable."

"Those places are horrible. I had a room like that…" his voice drifts off as his eyes wander past me. "I mean I used to keep a room like that for when I… I sometimes went there."

It was a fuck pad. The fact that his face is flushed confirms it. I've never thought of Ben in any sexual way and the inference that he kept a room just for fucking women makes me instantly uncomfortable. There's no denying he's gorgeous but I don't want the imagined image of him in bed floating through my thoughts. "I get the picture."

"Why don't you stay with me and Kayla?" He leans back in his chair. "We've got two extra bedrooms. I know she'd love having you there."

I believe him. I met Kayla briefly yesterday when I stopped by the Foster Foundation's office in the financial district. I was surprised she was working on a Saturday morning until she explained everything she had on her plate. I told her I'd help in any way I could and the relief in her expression was almost palpable. I could tell instantly that the kindness that radiated from her was one of the reasons Ben was so deeply in love with her.

He drums his long fingers across his thigh. "I don't want you staying at a hotel, Lilly. You should get your stuff and come to our place tonight."

The part of my heart that wants the reassurance that there's still a place where I belong in the world is chomping at the bit to take him up on his offer. The realistic parts of me are screaming that it's a bad idea. Ben has helped me through some of the worst moments of my life but there's always been an arm's length of emotion between us. We're close in many ways but in fundamental, day-to-day life stuff, we're not that familiar with one another. Intruding on the space he shares with the woman he loves isn't something I want to do. I don't want to jeopardize the friendship we have. I can't. It's the only thing that is holding me together at this point.

I open my mouth to respond just as the waiter approaches the table to refill Ben's wine glass. I shake my head slightly when he asks if I want another sparkling water. He nods in acknowledgement as we both listen to Ben answer his smartphone. I stare at him as one medical phrase after another falls effortlessly from his lips. He survived a horrible loss and now his life is exactly where he wants it to be. I want that too. The only difference is that I have no idea how to get my life on a track towards a happy future.

Chapter 4

Ben had insisted on riding the subway with me back to my hotel. The moment he realized that we were crossing into Queens, he'd started on a path of trying to convince me to pack up my stuff and go home with him. As inviting as the offer is, I won't change my mind. As we took the elevator up to my floor, I promised him that if I didn't have a job within the week that I'd move in with him and Kayla temporarily. It was enough to appease his anxiety. It was also enough to give me the breathing room I need to evaluate my next move.

I breathe a heavy sigh as I glance down at my smartphone. The text message that just flashed across the screen is from Rowan Bell, Clive's assistant. We'd been volleying messages back and forth the past few days. She wants me to either stop by the office to pick up my first and only paycheck or she wants my current address so she can mail it to me. There's no right way to respond to her because I know that there's a strong chance that Clive will use my decision to his advantage. Walking back into Corteck's corporate offices would be a brutal reminder of my lost dream and giving her the address of my hotel will mean he'll know exactly where I am. I need the money too much to ignore her any longer.

I tap out a quick message asking if she can have an envelope ready for me to pick up at the main reception desk tomorrow. I know that it's doubtful that I'll be able to exit the building without having to face Clive, but at least in the crowded lobby, I have a chance of getting out with my emotions intact.

She responds almost immediately with a text saying that will be fine.

I don't look at my phone again before I crawl into the bed. I turn on the television hoping the noise will block out the muttered hums of the arguing couple in the room next door and I drift into a much needed sleep.

***

"Ms. Bell said that there would be an envelope here for me."
I tap my fingers on the edge of the steel counter for good measure.

"I told you, there's nothing." The same receptionist who had
tried to get rid of me the day I met Rowan is staring a path through
me. "You should call her and ask her what's up with that."

Really? This is the face of Corteck?

I smile inwardly as I think about how many people who
come into the lobby are greeted with this. "Isn't that your job?"

She pushes her hands against her keyboard and I wonder
briefly if she's about to stand so she can slap me across the face.
"Fine," she spits out so violently that saliva sprays across the desk.

I take a step back. I avoided that first assault and I can't be
certain that there won't be another. "Tell her that Lilly Randall is
here," I say the words before I realize that Rowan may actually know
my birth name. My initial impression of her was that she and Clive
are close. They had to be for her to have known about Parker, his
half-brother. I suddenly feel self-conscious and regretful that I didn't
just give her the address to the hotel I'm staying at.

"She'll be right down." She gestures with her chin toward a
row of chairs I'm all too familiar with. I'd camped myself there for
hours on end while I waited to see Clive right after I'd graduated
from MIT. The irony of the situation isn't lost on me as I settle into
one to wait for Rowan to bring me the only money I'll ever earn
working for the company of my dreams.

I hear the sound of his footsteps across the marble floor
before the first trace of his cologne hits me. I knew that there was a
strong possibility that he would be the one I'd have to talk to when I
got on the train this morning to come back into Manhattan. I haven't
forgotten his pointed words about the two of us not being done. I
scrub my hand over my face just as his shoes come into my field of
view.

"Lilly," he says in a low growl. "I'd like to see you in my
office."

"Do you have my paycheck, Mr. Parker?" I look up into his
face marveling at how in control he looks even when his hair is
slightly disheveled.

"I'm having it brought to my office," he counters as he
reaches out his hand towards me. "We can talk there."

The fact that I need the small amount of money I've earned here is the only thing that is making me consider his proposition. I don't want to talk about what happened the last time I was in this building. I don't want him to understand the constant pain that gnaws at the deepest parts of me. I've shown him too much of my heart already but the fact that I need to pay for the room I'm renting is enough to bring me to my feet. "I only have a few minutes."

"That's all I need," he says in a muted whisper as he places his hand on the bottom of my back to lead me through the lobby to the bank of elevators that will take us to the thirty-seventh floor.

Chapter 5

"Thank you," I offer as I reach to take the bottle of chilled water from him. I hadn't hesitated when he'd asked me if I wanted anything to drink. My mouth is bone dry from the anxiety that is surging through me. He didn't say a word to me on the elevator. The fact that there were three other people on the lift may have been the reason, but it hardly mattered. I knew that there was no way he was going to delve into the subject of what happened last Tuesday in this office in front of anyone else. Clive Parker is too private a man to wave his dirty laundry in anyone's face.

"Rowan has your paycheck, Lilly," he begins before he stops to nod towards the closed door of his office. "I'll call her in to bring it to you but I want to discuss a few things first."

I can't say I'm surprised by his confession that he wants to talk to me. I knew when I saw him at the library that he would need to speak his mind before I'd be rid of him for good. I can act like a stubborn brat and postpone the inevitable to another day or I can try to grin and bear it now. I'm the one who opened the can of worms that I threw right at his head. I shouldn't have tossed out the details about my family at him, even if I was trying to defend my honor. It's a subject I don't bring up for good reason. "What do you want to discuss?"

He pulls at the fabric of his pants before lowering himself in the chair next to mine in front of his desk. He faces me directly, drawing in a deep and measured breath. "I'm very sorry about what happened to your family and to you."

I've heard the words before dozens of times. They were frequent and heartfelt in the days and weeks following the shooting. Over time, the gravity of their meaning has diminished as I've pulled myself together and moved forward into the world alone.

"I appreciate that, Clive." I don't look at him as I reply. It's not because I don't value the thought behind the sentiment. It's that I know if I do look at him I'll see sorrow and pity there. It's why I don't tell people about my past. The carefree and honest way they treat me inevitably shifts to something different once they know.

They view me as fragile or broken. I'm not those things. I may have been at one time but I'm not now.

"There are a lot of details online about what happened." I hear the audible sound of him swallowing hard. "It's a miracle you survived."

The doctors had told me the very same thing when I was taken to the hospital after the shooting. The bullet had entered my neck at an extreme angle before it lodged in my flesh. It hadn't caused any lasting physical damage. The ongoing trauma from that night is the knowledge that I ran through the house after the gunfire stopped. I saw every person I loved bleeding to death and I had to call 911 before I collapsed. Those images never escape me. They linger with me just as the scar at the base of my hairline does.

"I feel very badly about some of the things I said to you the other day." His fingers scurry over the edge of his knee catching my eye. "I had no right accusing you of anything."

It's a start. It's also an end. Listening to Clive explain away his ruthless behavior isn't going to change a thing. The man arranged for me to be out of the apartment I was living in so he could acquaint himself with my personal computer files. It's a violation of trust that I'll never get over and regardless of what he says to me, it's not going to change the fact that working for him is no longer my one and only career goal.

Closing my eyes briefly, I pull all the composure I can find from within before I look at his face. "You had no right to go through my personal computer."

"You signed a document when you..."

I pull my hand into the air to ward off his words. "I signed a document and then I slept with you. You made me feel special. I don't know if you regularly do that with your new recruits or not."

"I don't, Lilly." He shakes his head faintly. "What happened between us has nothing to do with my looking at your computer."

It's a laughable statement but I'm too angry to find the humor in it. "It has everything to do with it. You violated me."

"I know it feels that way." I can hear a note of sincerity in the words. "I've trusted people in the past who have fucked me over."

I trusted a man last week who fucked me over. I'm looking right at him.

"You wanted me to live with Rebecca so you would have access to my computer," I spit the words out with all the distaste the notion carries with it. "You had it planned right from the start."

"No," he murmurs. "I wanted you to live with Rebecca because I knew she'd look out for you. You're young and this city isn't always kind to women like you."

He's slapped another label to me. In addition to being young, now he thinks I'm naïve and unable to care for myself. I push because I need to. I have nothing left to prove to him, other than the fact that he's wrong about my ability to take care of myself. My past is proof enough of that. "Women like me? What does that mean?"

He pinches the bridge of his nose. I can tell the conversation isn't going in the direction he wanted it to and I feel a jolt of relief over that. Clive likes to be in control. The symmetrical alignment of everything on his desk is evidence of that fact. I saw it when I was in his apartment too. He needs and wants to dictate every aspect of his life, including discussions and this one has gotten away from him. "You're taking it the wrong way, Lilly. Please don't."

"It doesn't matter how I'm taking it, Clive." I pull on the neckline of the green dress I'm wearing. I don't want the top of my bra to sneak into view. Giving Mr. Parker a peep show is part of my past. After today, I'll never have to worry about flashing the man again.

"When we went out for dinner a couple of weeks ago," he stalls as his eyes focus on my hands and my desperate measure to keep myself covered. "Do you remember when we went out for dinner a couple of weeks ago?"

"I remember," I say quietly. I don't want to delve back into the fact that we briefly dated for a few hours. Our personal relationship blew up the moment he took the liberty of turning on my laptop. "It was a mistake."

His gaze narrows as he leans forward in his chair, resting his elbows on his thighs. "That wasn't a mistake. The mistake was when I invaded your privacy."

In terms of apologies, it's not the most obvious one I've ever received. I've been craving it though so I'm going to unwind his words and take comfort in the fact that he realizes that what he did was wrong. "That was more than a mistake."

"Lilly." His hand juts out towards me. He stops it before it brushes against my knee, pulling it back into a fist on his lap. "When we were at the restaurant, there was something about the way you smiled at me. I…"

"I was having a good time." It's not a lie. I remember the night fondly. It felt as though we had connected on a level that transcended work. He'd told me stories about when he was in college and he'd listened intently to mine. The man I had dinner with that night was a man I wanted to have dinner with every night. I'd started to fall for him and I thought the same sentiment was there, reflected back to me in his eyes.

"I don't think there was a man in the restaurant who didn't stare at you." His voice hardens. "I can't blame them. I had the same reaction when I first saw you in Boston at the bistro."

Flattery is welcome but not if it's coming from a place of desperation. Guilt is driving him to say the things he's saying. The fact that he can't look me in the eyes speaks more than any of his words ever could. "None of this matters anymore. Can you get Rowan to bring my paycheck?"

He glances down at his wristwatch. "I'll call her soon. I need you to understand something. It's very important."

It's not important. At least to me it's not. I don't know how anything that he says can be relevant to my life at this point. I don't work for him. I'm not sleeping with him again. My connection to Clive Parker is over for good. "I just want to go."

"I wanted you to live with Rebecca because I knew she'd keep an eye on you." He slowly pulls his hardened fist over his thigh. "I admit I did it for a selfish reason."

He admits being selfish? It's not as though it's an epiphany that will alter my view of him.

"I get that you wanted that control over me." I look at his office door, willing it to open so Rowan can walk through it with my paycheck in her hand. "You wanted access to my computer and getting me to live with your best friend gave it to you."

"I did want control." His voice is deep as he leans forward, catching both my hands in his. "It had nothing to do with your computer."

I stare at my hands and how small they look within his. "What then? What are you talking about?"

"I wanted you to live with her because I knew you'd be safe there." He squeezes both my hands in his. "There's a reckless side to you, Lilly. You shared way too much with my brother. I was worried about what you'd do once you got to New York. I just wanted Rebecca to watch out for you."

"What exactly does that mean?" I push because some clarification is what I desperately need.

"You were willing to share nude photos of yourself with Parker. You didn't know him," he says hoarsely. "Doing shit like that in New York can land you in a completely different kind of mess."

Chapter 6

The man has one of the most brilliant minds in technology today. He runs a company that some have estimated to be worth billions of dollars. He's cultured, refined and sophisticated. He has dated beautiful women for most of his adult life and he can get laid with a snap of his fingers. Yet, he wants me to believe that he arranged for me to live with one of his dearest friends because he thought I'd hand out nudie photos of myself in Times Square? The man has pegged me as an idiot if he thinks I'm falling for that bullshit.

I pull my hands free of his even though I feel bereft when I do. My body is betraying my desire to race away from him. "You're telling me that you wanted me to live with Rebecca because I sent one naked picture of myself to a man who happens to be your brother?"

"You sent a naked picture of yourself and a letter about sucking cock."

I pull my hands up to my face. "I did it once. I was trying to have some fun. There was no harm in it."

"No harm?" He clenches his hand into a fist. "What if someone else would have seen it, Lilly? A picture like that can impact your entire future."

I know that. The thought has crossed my mind time and time again since I sent it. "I would never do it again."

"You shouldn't have done it the first time," he spits back.

I study his face. I can tell he's frustrated. "I regret doing it. I know I'm lucky that no one else saw it."

"You're damn right you're lucky." He tips his chin towards the floor. "I destroyed it and that letter so no one will ever see it."

I should thank him for doing that for me but right now I can't twist my mind away from the anger I'm feeling. "You haven't trusted me since I sent that stuff to Parker. That's why you really wanted me to live with Rebecca."

"You're wrong." He leans back in his chair again, leisurely crossing his legs. "I wouldn't have offered you the job if I didn't trust you."

"Rowan offered me the job." I point out. "She saw the value in my education and my drive."

He cocks a dark brow as he studies my expression. "You don't think I see the value in those things, Lilly?"

I don't know how to logically answer that question. I want to believe that he was being honest when he told me that I was the smartest woman he ever met. Now, I don't know what is real and what is based solely on his desire to confirm his suspicions about me. "I think that you honestly thought I was going to use your family's name to market the organ donation app I've developed. I think you looked through my computer because something inside of you didn't trust me."

His chin drops and his shoulders surge forward as he exhales. "I didn't go to see Rebecca that morning with the intention of looking at your computer."

The strength of the declaration pushes me back in my seat. I lean back into the leather chair, trying to decipher exactly what he just said to me. "That's a lie, Clive."

"Have you spoken to Rebecca since that day?"

It's a question that is rhetorical to me. He already knows the answer to it and I'd bet my paltry life savings on that. "You know I haven't. You've asked her if I've called her, haven't you?"

He rolls his eyes towards the ceiling. I can see his exasperation mounting with each passing moment. I'm not going to back down from this because, at this point, I have nothing to lose. I don't work for the man anymore and I'm never crawling back into bed with him.

"You arranged to have me meet Jordan here that day to look over your security files," I stop as I poke my finger in the air towards him. "You didn't care what I thought about those files. It was an excuse to get me down here so you could look at my computer."

His hand dips into the inner pocket of his suit jacket to retrieve his smartphone. I watch in silence as he scrolls his finger over the screen before he brings the phone to his ear. "Jordan, come to my office. Now."

***

"I heard that you quit." Jordan smiles at me as she takes Clive's place in the chair next to me. "What are you doing back here?"

I can't shield my surprise over the fact that she looks genuinely happy to see me. "I came to get my paycheck."

"I was shocked that you'd left." Her gaze darts up to scan Clive's face before it settles back on me. "I was worried about you. We had a dinner date last Tuesday, remember?"

I had remembered on Wednesday. By then the idea of texting or calling her to explain why I was a no-show seemed useless. She's a part of the Corteck family, which means she likely reports back on everything she does to Clive. If I had called her to apologize for not making it to her place, he would have heard about it immediately. I have no doubt about that. I can't imagine that anyone can work for Clive for long before they are doing his biding for him. I have to admit that the notion that Clive had instructed her to befriend me so he could gain more information about me had crossed my mind. I wouldn't put it past him.

"I'm sorry I didn't call," I offer as an expected apology, not because it's something that I truly mean.

"My husband's friend still wants to meet you." She holds up her smartphone. "I showed him a picture I took of you when we were working together on the security system. He's been harassing me for your number ever since."

I blush at the admission. The only person I have to hang out with in New York is Ben and our relationship is based solely on the fact that we are connected through grief. I thought that Clive could fill in the empty space I feel but that's not going to happen. "I'll take his number. I can call..."

"Lilly is involved." Clive crosses his ankles as he leans back against the edge of his desk. "Tell your husband's friend it's not going to happen."

I'd be touched by the territorial tone of his voice if I felt anything beyond frustration and disdain for him.

"He's wrong." I gesture with my chin towards Clive. "I'm not involved. You can give him my number."

We both turn to look at Clive in unison when we hear the muted curse he says beneath his breath.

"I have to go, Jordan." I pull myself up. "It was nice to see you again."

"Sit down, Lilly." Clive nods towards the chair I was just sitting in. "I asked Jordan to come here because I want her to explain what's going on with the security system."

I don't sit back down because I have no interest in hearing anything either of them has to say. "I don't work here anymore," I point out through a clenched smile. "Your security system isn't relevant to me."

The shadow of a grin catches the corner of his mouth before he looks down at Jordan. "Explain to Lilly what we discovered after looking over her notes."

Jordan scratches the back of her head. I see the hesitation in her eyes as she looks at him. "She doesn't work here anymore, Clive."

"Tell her," he pulls an extra syllable out of each word as if that will grant them more meaning.

She nods in agreement. "We realized after looking over the notes you made that there was a potential breach point."

I don't move from where I'm standing next to Clive. My eyes are centered on Jordan. "I'm glad I could help," I say with more sarcasm than I intend to.

"Two of the computers being used by the researchers needed an operating system patch." She glances at the floor briefly before pulling her gaze back to me. "We assumed it was taken care of weeks ago but you caught the issue immediately. It was an important find, Lilly."

It was an incredible find given the security that is in place at Corteck. It stuck out like a sore thumb to me and I'd mentioned it to Jordan at the time. She'd shrugged it off as being a simple oversight but judging by the stern expression on Clive's face now; it's an issue that could have had far reaching consequences.

"You can go." Clive moves swiftly towards the door of his office and I immediately follow suit.

"I'll just go to Rowan's office to get my paycheck," I mutter under my breath as I breeze past him.

I feel his hand grab my elbow just as I'm about to walk over the threshold into the hallway. "You're not going anywhere."

Chapter 7

"When are you going to realize that you're wasting your time?" I tap my shoe against the floor-to-ceiling window as I look down on the bustling streets of Manhattan. "I just want my money so I can go."

"We're not done, Lilly." His breath hovers over my neck. "I'm not letting you walk out of here until you understand a few things."

I edge to the side to avoid being trapped between his arms. I don't want a replay of what happened the night of the office party. My body is longing for it but my mind is in control and it's telling me that Clive Parker is the biggest mistake I've ever made. "I don't need to understand anything. Why can't you just let this go?"

"This?" His hand flies through the air to hover over my head. "You?"

I clasp my hands together in front of me. "I don't want to be here anymore. I'd like to leave."

"Did you like spending time with me?"

It's a ridiculous question considering the magnitude of what's transpired between us the past few days. "I'd like to leave," I repeat.

"I told you that I've never met anyone like you, Lilly." He steps closer and out of sheer need, I step back to widen the distance between us even more.

"I don't think I've ever met anyone as merciless as you." The words are filled with child-like spite and spirit but I'm past the point of caring whether I appear to be a mature adult or not. "The stuff that people say about you online is true."

He tips his chin towards me. "You've researched me."

There's no denying that it's a statement without any curiosity behind it. I'm assuming he's jumped to that conclusion based on the fact that I had tried desperately to get a job with Corteck for years. "I wanted to work here. I knew that if I had a better grasp of your background that it would give me a leg up."

"I'm not talking about that." He crosses his arms in front of him, before he raises his left thumb to his lip. "I'm talking about the browser history on your computer."

The man has no sense of decency at all. His lame attempts to convince me that he just happened to be visiting Rebecca when he saw my computer aren't buoyed by this latest confession. "You actually looked at my browser history when you were helping yourself to my computer files?"

He steps forward again, lessening the space between us. I don't back down this time. I feel my heart pounding. I'm livid. The added knowledge that he took the time to open my browser and rifle through my search history has me bordering on full-on rage. I'm sure that a quick glance in the mirror would confirm the fact that my face is actually turning red from all the fury I feel racing through my body.

I can sense that he's struggling to find the right words. His tongue darts over his bottom lip, moistening it. "No. I'm talking about the computer you used here."

I feel my jaw clench. I can't control my reaction. "Shit."

"Let's see." He leans down so his breath floats over my forehead. "Clive Parker girlfriend was one search term. Clive Parker dating was another. Age of the women Clive Parker dates."

I pull my hand over my mouth to muffle the internal scream that I feel is about to escape from me. I remember sitting at my station during lunch one day and doing a search of all things Clive Parker. I'm too smart to be doing shit like that. I know for a fact that I deleted my browser history but at Corteck, it wouldn't take anyone more than twenty seconds to retrieve that information. "Fuck."

"You were interested in me, Lilly."

I run my index finger over my left eyebrow. "I was."

"You still are." His hand leaps to my hip.

I step back far enough that it drops to his side. "I'm not anymore."

"I want to fix what happened between us."

"You can't." My eyes shoot to the door of his office. I need to leave. I have to get away from him now.

"I fucked up." His hand darts back towards me and I almost stumble as I move back quickly.

"I can't be here anymore." I reach into the air to grasp something to level myself.

His hand catches mine. "Please don't go. I need you to stay."

I look down to where my feet are now planted firmly on the

floor. I wrench my hand free of his. "Mr. Parker, I don't work here anymore. I'm not sleeping with you again. I want my money so I can leave. "

He doesn't say another word to me as he pulls his smartphone from his pocket. He runs his thumb over the screen and tells Rowan to bring my paycheck to his office.

Chapter 8

"So you're the wonder kid I've been hearing about?" His green eyes lock on mine. It's rare for me to meet anyone with the same shade of eyes as me. There's a strange kinship there that I doubt he's feeling. The man, after all, is Alec Hughes.

"Mr. Hughes." I look down at the red pencil skirt I'm wearing. "I want to thank you…"

"Never call me that, Lilly." He taps the end of his pen against his desk. "I'm Alec. You're going to call me Alec. You got that?"

I smile at the stern reminder of his name. "I've got that."

He picks up a piece of paper that has been sitting atop a massive pile of magazines on the corner of his desk. "My assistant, Lance, tells me that you weren't taking any prisoners during your interview. It's all anyone around here is talking about."

I blush. I never expected to be called in for a second interview at Hughes Enterprises. I had actually applied at several diners yesterday with the hope that I could get something to help me move out of the hotel and into an apartment. "I was just trying to clarify what the position entailed."

"You practically invented a new position for yourself." He raises both brows. "Actually, technically, you did."

I lean forward. I try hard not to read between the lines but these lines hold the promise of something that may wash the memory of my brief stint at Corteck out of my mind. I ask the obvious question. "What position?"

"I've been looking to branch out more in the app market." He pushes his hands against the arms of his chair. "It's a space we need to have more of a presence in. I think you can bring that to the table for us."

My heart wants to leap at the idea of doing what I love the most and getting paid for it, but I'm hesitant after what happened at Corteck. I press for more while I try to contain my ever growing excitement, "I'm not sure I understand what exactly you're looking for. Are there specific apps that you're considering developing?"

"I downloaded that medical travel app you're selling." He nods towards his smartphone, which is sitting directly in front of him on the desk. "It's a work of art, Lilly. Your brain is in a league of its own. I want you to be at the helm of new app developments for us. You'll work mainly on your own coming up with ideas and then our senior team will help work out the kinks."

These are the words I craved to hear from Clive Parker when I first walked into his office. I can sense the excitement in Alec's voice. He sees the value I'm bringing to the table and for me, that's not going to translate into just a steady income, but it's going to allow me the freedom to work on the projects that I see the most value in.

"Your resume says that you've worked primarily in a bistro." He cocks a brow. "Do you have any experience beyond that? I know you're developing stuff on your own but I'm wondering about anything related directly to what you'd be doing here."

"I worked for Corteck for a couple of weeks." I feel foolish admitting to my brief time at Clive's company but I need to be honest. I'd hate for that tiny bit of information to pop up months down the road. I want to be candid even if I have no idea how I'll explain why I left there.

"You worked for Clive?" His dark brow pops up. "That guy's something else."

I don't respond because I have no idea whether the something else he's referring to is a good or bad thing.

"What happened with that? Did he realize you were smarter than him so he let you go?"

I laugh out loud at the notion. "It was about a personal project I've been working on. I actually have a question about that if I may?"

"You may ask whatever you want." He waves his hands in the air. "I need you to work here so ask away."

I stare down at my palm for a moment. I need to ask if I want to start off on the right foot at Hughes Enterprises. "I'm just wondering if I'm allowed to work on my own projects on my off time. I have a lot of ideas for apps that I could help you develop but I'm working on a couple that are just mine."

The corner of his mouth pops up. "What you do after you walk out of this office every day is none of my business. I actually like that you have the drive to develop your own stuff. It shows how committed you are to your craft."

That's all I need to hear. "I'd really like to work here."
"Consider yourself part of our team, Lilly."

Chapter 9

"I can still help you and Kayla with whatever you need." I nod towards the bedroom of the small apartment I've rented in Murray Hill. "I mean I want to volunteer my time to help you."

"You don't have to do that, Lil." Ben heaves the heavy suitcase he's carried up three flights of stairs over his shoulder. "Your clothes weigh a fucking ton."

I throw my head back in laughter. "They do not. You're not as strong as you think you are."

He stops to toss me a stern grimace. "That's not possible."

I mutter under my breath about how he needs to work out as I follow him down the short hallway to the bedroom. "I've wanted to talk to you about something since I got to New York."

"Do you want me to help you put some of this stuff away?" He nods towards the two suitcases that have been holding all of my worldly possessions since I left Rebecca's apartment. "Or do you want to handle that yourself?"

It's a kind gesture that speaks of the vaguely familial relationship that we share. After inadvertently modeling most of my underwear collection to Clive Parker, I'm trying to keep it under wraps. The thought of Ben seeing anything personal of mine creates an instant knot in the pit of my stomach. "I'll put it all away later. Can you sit and talk for a bit?"

"Sure, Lil." He pulls on the bottom of the white t-shirt he's wearing before he sits on the edge of the bed. "You look worried. Did something happen?"

It's the doctor part of him talking. Ever since I first met Ben he's worn the same look of concern on his face whenever his inner instinct tells him that I'm struggling with what happened to my family. When he initially suggested that we spend time as friends outside of the grief counseling group, I was hesitant. I had shut myself off from the entire world. I rarely spoke to my maternal grandmother who took me into her home even though she could barely stand straight under the weight of her own grief.

I settle on the bed next to him, reaching to grab his hand. It's not the closeness that I crave but the stability.

"Lil." He pushes my hair behind my ear. "I can tell something isn't right. You have to tell me."

I glance up at his face seeing the broken man who confessed to me years ago that he felt it was his fault that his mother had died. Even though he was only a teenager when she had passed, he felt the need to shoulder the blame based on the fact that he hadn't checked the connections on her oxygen tank. She had drifted into death while he was in a guest house with a girl. Her death may have lacked the violence of my family's but the pain of her loss is just as deeply felt by him as my loss is felt by me. "It's time, Ben."

He glances down at my hand. I should expand on my words but I know there isn't a need to. He's been pushing me to take this step for years and each time I've gotten close, the part of me that can't completely let go of my mother and my siblings, pushes me back into myself. I've been clinging to this one part of my past because once I do let it go; I have to face the fact that my history is completely untethered. There won't be a place I can go to anymore. I'll have to make decisions that I haven't felt equipped to make until now.

"You've had a lot of change recently." He taps his finger on the white blanket that is spread across the bed. "Do you think this is the best time?"

I doubt if there will ever be a best time to sell the home that my family lived and died in. "I need to do it now."

"Why now?"

It's not the response I thought I'd get. Judging by the past and all the countless times that Ben pushed me to sell, I assumed he'd almost be jumping for joy. He's made it clear to me that he felt that keeping the house was hindering my ability to move forward. I've never viewed it that way.

"I'm building a new life for myself," I say it with all the conviction I feel inside. "I can't do that if it's still part of who I am."

He studies my face carefully. "I'm proud of you."

I smile at the words. I'm proud of myself too. Coming to this decision hasn't been easy but once I landed the job at Corteck and moved to New York I knew that it was time for me to face my past and put it and the people I loved most in the world to rest. "That means everything to me, Ben."

"I have a friend who works in real estate on Long Island." He straightens his long legs to pull his smartphone from the front pocket of his jeans. "I can call him and we'll get the ball rolling."

It's only one part of the puzzle. "I have to go there to pack up their things."

"Kayla and I will go with you." He pats his hand over my knee. "We won't let you do it alone."

I know they won't. I'm grateful for that. If I'm going to move forward in my life, this is the first, and most important, step I have to take.

Chapter 10

"Whatever Hughes is paying for you, I'll double it."

No, it's not Clive Parker saying those words to me, unless he has some odd strain of strep throat that's made him sound like a woman. It's Rowan, Clive's assistant. I'm standing in line at the sandwich shop across the street from my new office waiting to pick up my lunch. The fact that I'm blocks away from Corteck's headquarters shouldn't have given me the sense of ease that I've been feeling. It was inevitable that I'd run into someone who works there.

"How do you know I work at Hughes Enterprises?" I spin around on my heel.

She gestures with her hand towards the identification badge that's hanging from a lanyard around my neck. "I saw that when you walked in, Lilly."

My overly active imagination was convinced, for a very brief second, that she knew about my new place of employment because of one of those corporate spies that Clive is so paranoid of. "Right," I offer back out of a sense of embarrassment.

"I'm serious. I'll double what you're being paid now if you come back to Corteck."

I want to be buoyed by her words. The career driven part of me would love to believe that she's desperate to have me back at Corteck because they value my programming and developing skills. I know that's not the basis of her offer though. It has to be coming out of her sense of loyalty to Clive. "Why would you offer me that?"

I can tell that she's surprised by how bold my question is. Acting naïve might have played a part in my landing a job there in the first place, but I'm done with that now. All of Clive's cards are on the table right next to mine. I know his motivations and I'm convinced that her offer has more to do with his desperate need to win than anything else.

"You're a bright talent, Lilly." She looks past my shoulder as she says the words. "Clive and I both feel your future is at Corteck. We have a lot to offer you."

The only thing they can offer me is years of worrying about my personal files being compromised. I have no desire to step back into an environment in which my ideas are never truly my own. "I have a question."

"Sure." Her gaze finally settles on my face. "What is it?"

I see a flash of compassion there and I have to wonder whether Clive filled in the blanks about why I left. "Mr. Parker took it upon himself to look at some of the private files on my personal computer when I was working for him and I'm wondering if he kept a copy of those."

Her eyes dart down to my laptop bag which I've strung over my right shoulder. Since Clive told me he went through it, I've kept it as close to me as I can. I felt a profound sense of relief when I realized that I wouldn't have to grant access to my computer to anyone at Hughes Enterprises. Lance, Alec's assistant, had reiterated the fact that my life outside the office was my own.

"I didn't know about that." Her voice cracks as she says the words softly. "I'll ask Clive about that if you want me to."

"I'd appreciate that and if he has a copy, I'd like it since I'm not working for you anymore."

"Of course." Her hand jumps to my wrist. "I'm sorry, Lilly. I had no idea."

I can't tell whether she's being sincere or not. I don't bother to stick around to find out. I pull my hand free of hers as I brush past her and walk through the door and onto the crowded sidewalk.

Chapter 11

The faint knock of my apartment door pulls me up from the comfort of my bed. It's just past seven. I'd fallen between the covers right after I got home. Seeing Rowan earlier had thrown me into an emotional tailspin. I hadn't considered the notion that Clive may have kept a copy of my files until I heard myself explaining his actions to one of his closest associates. The emotional burden of that had pulled on every corner of me while I tried to power through my work this afternoon. By the time I got onto the subway, I was ready to sleep the night away.

The knock is louder the second time and I know that all I need to do to chase Ben away is send him a quick text telling him that I'm not feeling well enough to talk about the sale of my family home. The realtor he'd asked to handle the listing had come up with a fair asking price. All that was left was for me to go there to pack up all of the pictures, toys and mementos that symbolized the end of the lives of the people I loved. Putting off the inevitable isn't going to change what needs to be done. I'm the one who asked him if he had time to stop by to talk so I push open the dead bolt lock before I twist the door handle in my hand.

"Lilly." Clive is standing in front of me as I swing the door wide open. "You're here."

He took my words from me before I had a chance to say them. "I live here."

"I know."

"Why are you here?" I know the customary thing to say would be to invite him in. I don't want that. I want Ben to appear behind Clive for moral support.

"Can I come in?" His gaze darts behind me to the barren space that will eventually be my living room. Right now, all that is there is the one armchair and side table that the landlord believes justifies the furnished apartment rate he's charging me for.

"I'm expecting someone." I move to look past his shoulder towards the staircase that leads up to the third floor. I don't see Ben even though it's more than thirty minutes after he promised he'd be here. Having an emergency room doctor as your only friend comes with a lot of concessions including spur of the moment cancellations.

"I'll leave when she gets here."

I don't correct him because it's none of his business who I'm expecting. "Fine," I spit out through clenched teeth.

He turns on his heel the moment I close the door behind him. "Rowan told me that she saw you today."

"That's why you're here." I don't present it as a question because it's not worth wasting my time trying to gain insight into what he discussed with her. "How do you know where I live?"

He scratches his head right above his ear. "You called the doorman at Rebecca's building yesterday to get your mail forwarded here."

"Why would the doorman tell you that?" I push my back into the door. I wish I would have left it open. My apartment feels too small and confined for the two of us.

"He didn't tell me that." He pushes his hands into the pockets of his pants. "He told Rebecca. She was standing in the lobby when you called."

I had debated that decision over and over in my mind, before finally deciding that I had no choice. I thought I'd live with Rebecca for at least several months so I'd given her address to all the companies I still have to deal with regarding my parent's house. I couldn't have known that when I called the doorman there to ask him to send me the mail I hadn't collected yet, that he'd share all those details with my former roommate.

"Lilly." His eyes dart around the empty space. "Would you like to go somewhere else to talk? I'd prefer to sit down."

I feel a surge of relief at the words. "There's a coffee shop across the street. I can meet you there."

He glances down at his wristwatch as he closes the space between us. "What about the person you're expecting? I can wait if you need to see her first."

I step out of his way, holding open the door to let him walk through. "I'll see my friend another time. I'll be down in ten minutes."

Chapter 12

"How do you expect me to believe you?" I try to keep my voice at an even and controllable pitch. "You must have saved the files. I don't believe that you walked away from my laptop without saving a copy of them."

He hangs his head in his hands. "I didn't save the files, Lilly."

"How do I know you're telling the truth?" I clench my hands tightly together before pulling them into my lap.

His finger traces a trail around the lid of the paper coffee cup sitting on the table in front of him. "I'm not going to lie to you. Ask me anything. I won't lie."

I stare at the untouched cup of coffee he bought for me. I have a million questions for him but not one of them seems relevant now. I've moved on from what happened in his office and in his bed. I'm forging ahead with a new life for myself that includes an apartment and a job I never realized I wanted. Delving back into why he did anything doesn't carry any weight in the world I'm living in now. "I don't want to ask you anything, Clive. I just want your assurance that you didn't save anything you saw on my computer."

"I told you that I didn't go to Rebecca's apartment with the intention of looking at your computer. It just happened."

"It just happened?" I parrot back. "Just like when you called me to your office during the mixer and touched me? That just happened too, right?"

"No." His eyes catch mine over the table. "I planned that. I wanted you."

I don't know what compelled me to bring up that moment of intimacy. I feel embarrassed that I took as much pleasure from him as I did. I was so unashamed and raw when he touched me. I came while pressed against a window, my desire unfettered and exposed. He helped me discover passion that I never knew I had within me and it was all in pursuit of his desperate need to uncover my secrets. He's a master of manipulation whether he admits it or not.

"I still want you, Lilly." His words feel loud and misplaced in the small, almost vacant, coffee shop we're sitting in.

I laugh out of a desperate need to not let any of my other emotions rise to the surface. The man violated me in a way that shook me to my core, yet hearing him say he still wants me throws me completely off balance. I can't judge whether he's telling me the truth or not because I don't know him. "I don't know how you expect me to believe you, Clive."

"Let me prove it to you." His jaw twitches. "I'll do whatever it takes to prove to you that I want you, Lilly."

"Even if you could prove that you still want me," I start within a whisper. "I would never be able to trust you again."

"I fucked up." He exhales sharply. "I didn't plan on looking at your computer. I saw it sitting there and thought about Parker and I had to know."

"Parker?" I try to ask in an even tone. "What the hell does he have to do with this?"

"I hate that Parker saw that picture of you and read that letter you wrote about sucking my…sucking his…" He visibly winces with the statement. "I can't fucking stand that he saw your body and read those words."

We haven't talked about Parker in weeks. I didn't consider him a relevant part of our relationship. He was the reason we met, but beyond that he is nothing to me, and judging by the fact that Clive had sent him across the globe with a one way ticket, I imagine he feels the same way about his brother as I do. "Why are you bringing up Parker?"

"I was worried there were more like him." He breathes out, closing his eyes briefly. "After we fucked, I couldn't stand the thought of another man seeing your body or touching you. I looked at your laptop to see if you had any pictures of other men or if you were emailing anyone like Parker."

He could be making all of this up to cover his tracks. He has no shortage of women waiting in the wings to jump all over him. Even the barista, behind the counter in this tiny coffee shop, has been eyeing him up since I sat down. "You don't strike me as the jealous type, Clive. You sleep with a different woman every week."

He sags back into the chair. I sense the words sting but they're the truth. He wants me to believe that he was so worried that I'd sleep with another man that he decided to go through my computer? The mere fact that his fishing expedition ended with him viewing the files related to the organ donation app I'm developing prove that he was went above and beyond looking at my saved pictures and emails. The man was on a mission to find something to throw in my face and he did.

"I haven't slept with a woman since I saw you at the bistro." His voice deepens. "I have no desire to fuck anyone else. I want to be with you, Lilly. You're going to tell me how I can make that happen."

Chapter 13

"Why are you doing this?" I take a sip of the now cold coffee from the paper cup before I place it back down.

"Doing what?" He cradles his own cup in his hand without bringing it to his lips. "What exactly do you think I'm doing?"

I should have an answer ready at the edge of my tongue to spit out at him, but I don't. "I just don't understand why you haven't dropped this. I don't work for you anymore. I'm not going to steal any of your ideas or secrets away. Why do you keep bothering me?"

"You think I'm bothering you?" A weak grin races over his lips. "I call it pursuing what I want. I suppose we just see it differently."

"You don't really want me, Mr. Parker." The formality feels natural to me even after everything we've shared. "I know that this is about something else."

"It's about my desperate desire to fuck you again, Lilly." He doesn't temper his tone at all. "It's more than that though. I've never met anyone like you. I want to know you. I want to spend time with you."

He wants something that is buried just there below the surface where I can't see it clearly. "Is this still about the organ donation app?"

"The app?" His brow furrows. "I told you that I was sorry I'd jumped to the conclusion I had about that."

"What's going to happen if I decide to move forward with it and bring it to market?"

"I would hope that it would become the success I know that it has the potential to be." He rakes his hand through his hair. "It's only the tip of the iceberg for you, Lilly. You're going to do amazing things in your career."

"You're not going to have a team of lawyers at the ready to sue me for some sort of infringement on your sister's memory?" The words sound harsher than the intention that is fueling them. I'm not bitter. I'm simply trying to gain a sense of understanding about where his head really is.

"I will do whatever I can to help you make the app a success. You can use any of my resources." He taps his finger on the edge of the table. "I mean it, Lilly. It's an important undertaking and I know that it's going to make a huge difference in the lives of many people. I'll do what I can to make it happen for you."

I tilt my head to the side to run my hand through my hair in a thoughtless attempt to gather my emotions together. I don't hear or sense any ulterior motive brewing behind the words. He sounds honest and genuine but this is Clive Parker. The man has already proven to me that he can manipulate me in ways I don't see coming. "Would you sign something guaranteeing that you won't sue me over this?"

His shoulders jerk back suddenly. "I don't have any legal right to sue you, Lilly. I'm sorry I threatened you with that."

I feel relief wash over me but the question is still there, lingering in the air between us. "Would you sign something?"

"I will sign anything you want me to." He leans forward in his chair, his hand skimming gently over the top of mine. "I want to protect you, Lilly. If I can prove that to you in any way, I'll do it."

***

"Can I ask you something before you go up?" His hands are tucked into the pocket of his pants, his suit jacket hanging open. "Would that be okay?"

I glance at the door to my building a few feet away. Even though Ben had texted me more than an hour ago apologizing for having to cancel our plans for the night, I hadn't told Clive that. He's still under the impression that I'm in a rush to get home because I have a friend stopping by. The truth is that I'm in a hurry to get upstairs so I can think within the peace that is my apartment. I need to process everything he said to me tonight and I can only do that if I'm by myself.

"What do you want to ask me?" I toss the question at him as I fumble in my large purse for my keys.

"How do you do it?" He sucks in a deep breath before he continues, "I mean, how do you manage as well as you do?"

I stop what I'm doing to look up at his face. I catch the pain that is there the moment his eyes lock on mine. I know what he's asking. I can see it there, hiding behind the sheltered veil of control that is always at the surface of his demeanor. "Do you want to come up for a few minutes?"

"I do." The rasp in his voice catches me off guard. "Please let me."

Chapter 14

"She died more than ten years ago." He teeters on the edge of one of the stools that sits next to the counter in my small kitchen. It's the only spot, other than the bedroom, where I can carry on a comfortable conversation with him.

"You miss her a lot," I say because it's what I see every time I look at him. I know the face of grief. It stares back at me from the mirror on my bathroom wall every day when I'm readying to go to work.

He picks up the glass of water I set on the counter after we'd arrived. I briefly doubted my decision to invite him into my apartment but knowing that he wanted to talk about his sister, I couldn't stop myself. I kept seeing Ben's face in my mind and the comfort that it always brings me when he listens to me talk about my family. Clive needs that and regardless of everything that has happened between us, we do share a common bond that I can't ignore.

"Have you ever met any of the people?" He swallows a large mouthful of water. "Ever since I found out about your family, I've wondered if you've met any of the people who received their..."

"Their organs," I finish for him. "I met two of them. It was years ago and we haven't stayed in touch."

He nods his chin towards my chest. "I see the woman who got Coral's heart all the time."

I've been able to connect the dots enough to know that. In a rare twist of fate, the woman who is raising Clive's nephew also happens to be the same woman who received his sister's heart after the car accident that took her life. "I can't imagine what that must feel like."

"I hate it," he murmurs. "I need it too. At this point we've become friends and I care about what happens to her."

"Is she like family to you?" I ask out of pure curiosity. I've tried to envision the same scenario in my own life time and time again but the situation is so far removed from my own reality that I can't piece it all together emotionally.

"Sadie's not exactly like family," he says with a faint shake of his head. "We both care about Cory, my nephew, and we both want what's best for him."

"You love him a lot, don't you?" I smile through the question. I first saw the tender affection Clive has for his nephew in his office when he told me he had to go see Cory because he was feeling under the weather. It sounded as though it was something as simple as a common cold, but the weight of worry was there, pushing on Clive's shoulders.

"He's the only family I have left." His voice is even and steady. "I have other family but they're not like Cory. I feel close to him."

"What about his mother?" I jump to clarify not wanting to assume anything. "Your sister is Cory's birth mother, right?"

"Christina." He fills in the blank effortlessly. "I have no idea where she is. She gave up custody of Cory to chase after her own dreams."

I had read a few articles online about Christina Parker. She's a few years younger than Clive and often popped up in searches related to him. She didn't seem to have any clear direction in life and I have to wonder if it's related to the fact that she'd been in the car the day Coral had been killed. She'd witnessed her sister's gruesome death first hand and I personally know the toll it can take. Judging her isn't part of my agenda.

"I want to know more about you, Lilly." His voice jars me from my thoughts. "I look at you and I don't know how you've accomplished everything you have after what happened to you."

I seriously debate how to respond. I've never liked talking about what happened that night six years ago. Giving voice to it always takes me right back to the moment when I heard my father walk through the front door of our home and methodically start his murderous rampage. "I try to stay focused on the future. I don't like thinking about the past."

"I can't let go of the past." His eyes flash over my face. "I admire you so much."

He says that because he can't see within me. He doesn't know that I'm so badly fractured that I'll never fully heal. I've had enough therapists tell me that the key to moving on is acceptance. It's easy for a stranger to toss that advice out when they have the comfort of a family's loving embrace to retreat to every night after a long day's work. All I have is the memory of my sister's screams, my mother's pleas and my father's vacant stare as he pulled the trigger over and over again.

"I'm trying to let go," I offer back. "I don't think it's possible to ever fully let go."

He leans back on the stool across from where I'm still standing beside the counter. "What if I don't want to let go of Coral?"

The words fall into the space between us and linger there. "I think you have to at some point, Clive."

"If I do that..." his voice trails as it cracks. He closes his eyes as he pulls in a heavy breath. "If I let go of her, no one will ever remember who she was."

I nod as I try to ward off the inevitable tears I feel flooding through me. "You'll always remember. It's impossible to forget."

Chapter 15

His hands cradle my face as he brushes a stray tear from my cheek with his thumb. "You understand what I feel, Lilly. No one ever has before."

"I know," I say out of a need to express something. He'd pulled me close to him after I started to cry. He didn't say a word. Instead he'd held me against his strong chest while I sobbed for what felt like endless moments. It couldn't have been longer than two or three minutes but the closeness is enough to remind me that I want more than I'm ever going to be able to have with him.

"I really want to kiss you." His eyes lock on my lips. "I've wanted to kiss you for days."

My body is craving the very same thing but if I give in to the want, I'll risk exposing more of myself to a man I'm not sure I can trust. "I can't kiss you."

His lips brush softly over my forehead. "I know that you can't."

I feel bereft at the words wishing in some way that he'd have pushed the issue more. My resistance is waning after listening to him talk about his family. I feel a connection to him that transcends the common denominator of the losses we've both suffered. "I'm tired. I think you should go."

I see his chest heave as he absorbs my words. I doubt that he thought that our deeply emotional conversation would lead to anything intimate. I feel as though I've been put through the paces of a triathlon race. I'm bruised and battered and in need of the comfort and solace of my lumpy new bed. I crave sleep and the escape it's always offered to me.

"Will you have dinner with me tomorrow?" He runs his thumb over my bottom lip. "Let me show you that I respect you, Lilly. Please give me another chance."

My better judgment wants me to tell him that there's no chance that anything will ever happen between us again. I know that it's the safe and logical thing for me to say to him but something has shifted. It may be because of his confession about not wanting another man to touch me. It's likely that it has more to do with our shared moment of grief. Regardless, I know that I'll regret it if I don't at least have dinner with him. "Dinner will work."

The corners of his lush lips pull up into a small grin. "I won't blow it this time."

"It's only dinner." I pull back from his touch. "I just want it to be dinner."

"Dinner is a start." He leans forward to kiss me gently on my cheek. "I'll pick you up at eight."

***

"Do you wear those at your new job?"

"Wear what?" I pull my gaze from the passing view outside the car window to look at him. My breath had caught when I'd walked about the front door of my apartment building to see him waiting in a navy blue suit. I doubt that I'll ever meet a man as devastatingly handsome as him again in my life.

"These." His hand brushes over my right leg, skimming the lace edge of the black thigh high stocking.

I push back into the car seat. I feel my cheeks flush at the knowledge that the driver sitting just a few feet in front of us could have easily gotten a glimpse of the top of my stockings when I slid into the car. I need to start looking down at my lap more.

"Do you dress like that when you go to work?" He can't contain his wide grin.

I twist slightly on my ass, giving me enough room to pull the hem of the dress back down to a decent level. "I wear them there, yes."

"Jesus." He shakes his head. "Thank Christ Hughes is getting married."

I can't help but laugh. I'd met the woman Alec Hughes is crazy about just yesterday. Libby Duncan is beautiful, kind and so welcoming that I'm already planning on going over to the condo they share for a home cooked meal next week. I've found a place at Hughes Enterprises where I not only fit, but I can flourish too. I love it there. "Alec is a great boss."

"Alec is a chump," Clive tosses back the words with a smile. "I had a chat with him the other day about you."

I shouldn't be surprised. Once Clive knew I was working for Alec I expected the two of them to discuss me. "Did Alec call you for a reference? I told him I worked for you briefly?"

"Alec did call me." He taps the leather of the seat between us. "He called me to gloat."

"To gloat?"

"He knows how talented you are." He studies the edge of his fingernails. "I told him he was lucky to have you."

"I'm lucky to work there." There's no malice in the words and I can tell from Clive's expression that he hasn't absorbed them that way at all.

"You're going to do great things for them, Lilly." He reaches to cup my hand in his. "I know that you are."

Chapter 16

"I want you so much." His lips push into mine, the sweet taste of wine lacing his tongue. "I'm so hard, Lilly. You can feel it, can't you?"

"Yes," I say into his mouth. I've felt his erection pressing against me since we arrived at his condo ten minutes ago. I agreed to come up under the guise of a quick brandy but I wanted more. I know that he can tell based on the way his hands have been cupping my ass. He has to know how wet I am already.

"All I think about is the way you taste. I crave the smell of your skin." He runs his lips over my neck, pushing my hair to the side. "I've never wanted a woman this much."

I weave my fingers into his hair, tilting his head so I can claim his mouth again. I deepen the kiss and I'm rewarded with a moan that escapes him and flows right into me. "I want this to be real."

He pulls back abruptly, his hands leaping to my shoulders, pushing me back into the wall. "This is real."

I study his expression trying to pull anything I can from it. "I can't tell if it is."

He takes a heavy step back. "You can't tell that I want you?"

My eyes drop to his crotch, the unmistakable outline of his thick cock pressing against the fabric of his pants. "I can tell that you want to fuck me."

He rakes his hand through his hair, a muttered litany of curse words falling from his lips in a heated rush. "It's more than that, Lilly. Christ. You can't feel it?"

I need to be honest. "I don't know what I feel. I'm confused."

He scoops my hand in his, bringing it to his moist lips in one fluid movement. "Come sit down. Let me tell you something."

I don't resist because I welcome the reprieve from the intensity I've felt since I got into the car with him earlier. We'd flirted shamelessly throughout dinner. I'd watched him staring at me while we traveled back to his place. I knew that he would kiss me the moment we stepped into the elevator as we made our ascent to his condo.

He motions towards a leather armchair. I rest my purse down next to it before I take a seat, carefully crossing my legs as I wait for him to speak.

"I hate that you work for Alec."

The words feel foreign in the context of what's transpired between us this evening. We hadn't spoken about my work since we arrived at the restaurant. "Why?"

"You're too good for them." He shifts back and forth, his shoes tapping out a rhythmic beat on the hardwood floors. "You should be working for Corteck."

It was inevitable that we'd be pulled back into this discussion at some point. I hadn't anticipated that it would be right now though. Not when we'd just shared a very passionate kiss. "I can't work at Corteck."

He slides his suit jacket from his shoulders allowing it to drop onto the couch behind him. "I know that you can't. I respect that."

"Why did you bring it up then?" I ask with an edge of regret. I don't want this conversation to spiral into the many reasons why I can't work for the man.

"I want what is best for you, Lilly." He moves closer to where I'm seated. "I only want what is best for you."

"You think that working for you is what is best for me, don't you?"

"No," he says as he leans forwards, his strong hands resting on the arms of the chair I'm sitting in. "I don't think it's best for you to work with me."

"You don't?" I cock a brow.

"If you wanted it, you'd have asked for your job back." His eyes scan my body. "I see how happy you are now that you're working with Alec. Why would I want to take that away from you?"

"I want to believe you," I say aloud even though I don't mean to. "I hope that you're telling me the truth."

"I'm losing money by not having you at Corteck." He closes his eyes briefly as he shakes his head. "You could have changed the entire app division. I have no doubt about that in my mind."

"Why haven't you tried harder to get me back?" They're the words a petulant child would say to a best friend who dumped them. I don't want to sound juvenile but I know, right now, I do.

"There is a job at Corteck for you whenever you want it." He leans down to graze his lips over mine. "I'd love to work with you again."

I nod. It's a generous offer and one I won't discount completely at this point. Right now, I'm finding my stride at Hughes Enterprises and I'm not changing that for anyone, not even for Clive. "I'll keep that in mind."

"I need you to trust me," he whispers the words into the still air between us. "I want you more than I've wanted anything in my life."

Chapter 17

The soft brush of his beard against my thigh pulls a shudder from deep within me. He's so close. I can feel his breath on my slick cleft. He's been teasing me for the past ten minutes, inching his lips and tongue down my nude body. I cried out when he bit my right nipple tenderly before blowing a puff of air across it. I moaned loudly when he circled the other with his tongue before pulling it between his lips in a soft, gentle kiss. Now, he's breathing on my sex and all I want is to feel his tongue graze over me. I know that it won't take much for me to come. I've craved his touch since the last time I was in this bed. "Clive, please."

"You'll come quickly, Lilly." His breath whispers over my flesh. "If you come, I'll want to bury my cock inside of you."

"I want that," I whisper. I do want it. As much as I know that I should have asked him to take me home, I couldn't resist when he'd fallen to his knees and kissed me in the other room. I was the one who pulled at his clothes to free his beautiful, strong body. I held his thick cock in my hands before he carried me to his bed and slowly stripped off my clothes.

"I want this to last all night." His tongue races over my inner thigh. "I want to lick this beautiful cunt for hours."

My hand drops to his hair. "I want to come."

He growls as I direct his mouth to the left. "You're so ready for me."

I cry out the moment his soft wet tongue touches my clit. I push my back into bed, arching my hips up towards him. He slides his hands under my ass, tilting my pussy so he can devour it easily and slowly.

"Yes," I hiss out between clenched teeth. I've been taken like this by men before but they've never been as skilled as Clive. "Right there."

He hones in on my clit, pulling it between his lips with the gentlest touch. He moans into me causing an extra wave of sensation to overtake me. I feel the rush of a climax barreling down on me.

"I'm going to come," I gasp into the air.

He pulls back slightly, his tongue expertly lapping at my folds. "You're so good. Christ, you taste so good."

I race to the edge, my hands pulling frantically on his hair trying to gain distance from him. I'm so sensitive and raw. I can't take the extra pressure of his tongue on me. "Please, oh, please."

"I'm not done," he purrs into my wetness. "I want to eat you for hours. I need this."

I push my head back into the pillow giving in to the overwhelming desire that he's pulling from me. I know I'll come hard again the second I feel his finger at my entrance. I scream his name as he slowly pushes two fingers into me. My breath stalls when I feel him touch a spot deep within me that pulls an uncontrollable need from within. I writhe beneath him, nothing existing in the moment but my desperate need to feel the pleasure he's giving to me.

I close my eyes as I finally feel my breathing level.

"Lilly." His moist lips are on my cheek now, his strong arms wrapped around me. "Sleep. Sleep here with me."

My voice is barely audible as I feel the softness of a blanket being draped over me. "I'll sleep," I whisper without opening my eyes. "I'll sleep."

***

"Can you have dinner with me again tonight?" His eyes race over my body as I step from the shower stall into the cool air.

I'd left him in the bed. I needed the comfort and time that a warm shower offered when I woke up in Clive's arms. I remember coming over and over again last night while he licked and tasted me. I fell asleep pressed against his chest and woke up in the exact same position. "You want to have dinner with me tonight?"

"Did you get water in your pretty little ears?" He reaches for another towel to dry my hair, pulling it softly across my ear. "I want you to have dinner with me tonight."

It's Friday and like every other night of the week my social calendar is empty. "I'm free tonight."

"Are you free tomorrow night?"

I look down to where he's now kneeling, drying my legs carefully. "You want to have dinner tomorrow instead of tonight?"

He flashes me a vibrant grin. "I want to have dinner with you every night for the next year. I'm going to ask you every day."

I smile down at him, soaking in the image of such a strong, brilliant man taking care of my most basic needs. "I'd like to have dinner today and tomorrow."

"What's your favorite kind of food?" He's on his feet now, adjusting the waistband of the pajama bottoms he must have put on before he came to find me in the shower.

"I like Thai food."

"I can't cook Thai food."

"I like Indian food too."

"I'll need a cook." He brushes his lips over my forehead. "Tell me what your favorite flower is."

"Why?" I look up into his eyes.

"I want to send you flowers one day and I'd prefer if they're the flowers you like most." He runs his hand over my hair. "I can brush your hair for you if you want me to."

I take a step back, my trembling hands reaching for the counter. "I can brush my hair."

"Lilly?" His hands leap to my cheeks. "What is it?"

He can't know. No one knows. "It's nothing."

He swallows hard. "It's your mother, isn't it? She brushed your hair for you?"

I nod, knowing that if I try to verbalize any response that it will come out swathed in a sob.

"Come here." He wraps his strong arms around me, pulling me into his body. "You don't have to be so strong. I can be strong for you."

I rest my head against his chest as I listen to his words and the strength of his heart beating within his chest.

Chapter 18

"You didn't tell me when I hired you that you tamed Clive Parker." Alec is leaning against the door to my office. "He's got great taste in flowers. I'll give him that."

I smile as my eyes flit over the beautiful bouquet of white lilies Clive had sent for me. The card delivered with them had brought an even broader grin to my face.

THEY'RE NOT AS BEAUTIFUL AS YOU. CLIVE XX

"Is it a problem that I'm dating him?" I ask just as the question floats into my mind. I hadn't thought about it because Alec and his assistant had both made it clear to me that they didn't care what I did on my off time. I'm sure neither of them would have imagined that I'd be dating one of their competitors.

"I can think of a dozen other guys who are better for you." He tips his chin towards me with a sly smile. "You're a sweet girl, Lilly. Just be careful."

I take the warning with a grain of salt. I know that almost everyone who has crossed paths with Clive views him as cold and heartless. I was part of that camp too before I realized that much of the aggression he presents to the world is a façade to cover the pain he's experienced over the death of his sister and the fall-out from that. The man who slept with me tucked in his bed last night has lived with loss for too long. I know that I can help him move forward just as he can help me.

"I'm working on that new shopping app we discussed last week. Do you want an update on that?"

"Don't tell anyone I'm about to say this…" His voice trails off as he takes a large step into my office, closing the door behind him. "You've come up with more ideas in the few weeks that you've been here than I've come up with in the past five years."

I laugh aloud at the confession. "I won't tell anyone."

"The week after next we're doing a media blitz day." He gestures toward the calendar hanging on the wall behind me. "We present a lot of new stuff that we'll be rolling out in time for the holidays."

I'm well aware of what he's talking about. Even though I've been happily serving coffee for the past few years, I've read every tech journal that is available. I've watched countless videos online whenever one of the major tech companies had an announcement. I know all about the importance of presenting what you have to offer to potential consumers before the competition does. "Are you thinking of launching one of the apps then?"

"I was thinking of launching the shopping one," he begins before taking a seat at one of the chairs near my desk. "I was wondering if you wanted the platform to present one of your personal apps."

I lean my elbows on my desk for support. "Are you asking me if I want to launch one of my own apps at your press event?"

"That's exactly what I'm asking you."

"Why would you do that?" I ask before I realize how ungrateful the question sounds. "I mean, it's such a generous offer."

"You are the future of programming, Lilly." He tilts his head to the side. "Everyone here agrees with me. If I can help you bring more attention to what you're developing personally, it brings more attention to the company as a whole. It's a win-win."

I scratch my neck, trying to decide my next move. "I do have an app that is very near completion. It's not something I'm going to market for profit. It's more a personal passion of mine."

"If you want, you can present it at our event."

"I always imagined I'd launch it quietly," I say aloud. "I just never imagined having a platform like that at my disposal."

"Get the shopping app ready to go and then use whatever resources you need here to get your own app set for launch." He nods towards my computer. "Take a day or two to give it serious thought. If you're comfortable with doing it, you can personally present both during our media day."

"I'll think about it."

"Good." He stands and walks back towards my office door. "Corteck always waits to plan their day until we've scheduled ours. They'll present on Thursday and we'll do Friday."

I smile knowing that his intention is to look out for me. "Thank you for the opportunity, Alec."

"Thank you for falling from the heavens into our tech division, Lil." He opens the door to step through. "You're our saving grace."

Chapter 19

"I don't think I can do it, Clive. Please."

"Sometimes, when I think about fucking this beautiful body." He positions himself above me. His bicep bulging as he balances the weight of his entire body on one hand. "I almost come on the spot."

I moan just as I feel the tip of his sheathed cock glide over my core. "I've already come so much. Everything is aching."

"You're swollen." He licks his lips as he stares down at me. "I love the taste of you. I would have eaten you again if you didn't push me away."

I had to out of sheer and desperate need. He'd pushed me onto my stomach after sliding my panties down. His thumb had pressed into my clit while he licked my pussy from behind. I'd come hard and fast before he started at me again. Now, the most sensitive parts of me are pulsing with an aching need. "I'm already so tender."

"That means you'll come harder when I fuck you." He pushes the lush head of his erection between my wet folds. "You're so wet for me. You're ripe and ready."

I moan at the words. He's right. I am ready. I've been ready since I arrived at his condo more than an hour ago. He'd kissed me gently and softly while I sat in his lap in the other room. I'd wanted to take him into my mouth but he wanted me more. He'd insisted on giving me pleasure. Now it's his turn to take pleasure from me. "I want it."

He pushes more of his cock into me and I let out a small, uncontrollable moan. The sensations are too much to hold everything in. I can't stop what I feel when he's taking me this way. He's larger than anyone I've ever been with and the gentle pull of pain that always comes when he's inside of me only deepens what I feel.

"Lilly." My name leaves his lips in a rush as he rams himself into me in one swift and fluid motion. "Christ, yes."

I try to reach for his hips, wanting to slow the rhythm. I don't want to come again already. I want it to last. I want to savor the gentle roll of his hips as he adjusts to how tight I am. I need to feel him pulsing inside of me. I have to hear the primal sounds he makes when he nears his own release.

"Clive." His name falls from my lips in a purr. "Fuck me."

His body stops as his hands dart to mine reaching to pull them over my head. "Say it, Lilly. Just fucking say it."

"Fuck me," I push it out slowly. "Fuck me hard."

"Jesus. That fucking sounds so sweet." He grinds his hips into me, pushing my entire body into the mattress with every thrust. "I'm so hard. I'm going to come so fucking hard."

I clench around him as I feel my own climax bearing down on me. I struggle against his hands, wanting him to let me go so I can claw at him. I need to feel him. "Let me touch you."

He lets go of my right hand and I grab onto his shoulder, grazing my nails across the hard flesh. He growls deeply, his cock pounding into me. "It's never been this good."

I race into an intense orgasm, my sex clenching around him. I call out his name, not caring that I can hear all the desperate desire I feel for him within it.

"Lilly." His lips find mine for a deep, lush kiss as his own release takes over his body.

***

"Will you have dinner with me tomorrow?"

It's the same question he asks me every day. I haven't turned him down yet but I have no choice given what I need to take care of tomorrow. "I can't tomorrow."

His head pops up from where he's been studying his laptop screen for the past thirty minutes. I'd busied myself with returning some work emails. I'm still not comfortable with the idea of having my computer in the same room as Clive. I don't believe that he'd compromise our connection in that way again, but I'm being wary. I have to be. "What are you doing tomorrow, Lilly?"

"I need to go to Long Island." I know that it's not enough of an answer to satiate his curiosity. Judging by the way he holds tightly to my hand whenever we're out on the streets of Manhattan, the territorial parts of him are on high alert. "It's some stuff about my family."

"I can go with you." His face brightens at his own suggestion. "I have that media thing, but I can get Rowan to handle it for me."

It's an offer that I couldn't have seen coming. I know how important the annual media day is to Corteck. I've read about their past projects and that day always provides the foothold they've needed to launch their products into success. Clive is the head of the company and as long as I've been following his career he hasn't missed one event. "You can't. It's too important."

"It's work." He snaps his laptop shut. "Come here and tell me what's going on tomorrow."

I pull on the hem of the t-shirt he gave me to wear as I pad across the floor to slide in his lap. He yanks me effortlessly onto the chair with him, wrapping me in his bare arms.

"Tell me, Lilly." He presses his lips against my cheek. "I want to know."

If I had any doubt about how much Clive Parker cares for me, it would all be erased right here and right now in this instant. I can feel the pounding of his heart against my side and I can sense the anxiety in his voice. "You must know by now that I was living in Suffolk County when my family died."

He nods briskly. "I did read that's where the shooting happened. Did you live there all your life?"

"No," I answer with no hesitation. "I was born there but we moved around a lot."

"Was it because of work?"

"I guess," I offer shakily. "My father wasn't happy in one place so he'd find a job and we'd move and then he'd find a new job and we'd move."

"You ended up back there when you were a teenager though?" The even tone of his voice is calm.

"Yes," I say quietly. "My parents decided to move back when my grandmother got sick."

"Is she alright now?"

I haven't spoken about her to anyone since her funeral. There were only a handful of acquaintances at the church that day. My grandmother had led a very quiet life and that was reflected in her death. She had retreated into her own world after my mother and siblings died. I was a reminder of what had been taken from her. I saw that whenever I traveled back to visit her. "She died last year."

His hand races over my hip to rest on my waist. "You've had so much loss."

I nod, not wanting the conversation to stall there. "We moved back because she was ill. My parents actually bought a house less than a block from where she lived."

"So you're going back there tomorrow to tie up some loose ends that your grandmother left behind?"

"I've taken care of all of that already." I had. My grandmother had left everything she owned to charity and her lawyer handled all the details for me. All I had to do was pick out the flowers and music for her short, unemotional service.

"What is it then?" he presses.

I reach towards my neck, my fingers edging over the fabric of the t-shirt. The necklace that once hung around my neck is gone now along with the comfort it used to bring me when I touched it. "I have to do something there."

"Lilly." He cradles my chin in his hand, arching my face up towards his. "Please tell me."

I nod, hoping that the simple movement will ward off the tears. "I need to pack up their things."

His brow furrows as he tries to piece together the fragmented mess I'm throwing at him. "Things?"

I can only manage a shallow breath before I speak. "I'm selling the house. I need to clean it out."

"You own the house that your family lived in?" There's no disguising the shock in both his expression and voice. "Someone hasn't taken care of that for you?"

I pat my chest. "They were my family. I need to take care of it."

"Christ, Lilly." He cradles my cheek in his palm. "Please let me help you with that."

As much as my heart wants that more than anything, I know it's too soon. It's a burden I don't want to place on his shoulders or my own. "My friends will help me."

"Someone is going with you?"

"My friend Ben and his fiancée are going with me. They'll help." I tell him. "I need to do this with them."

"I can be there if you need me to." He brushes my hair back from my forehead. "I'm only a phone call away."

Chapter 20

"I'd like to donate almost everything," I say as I stare at the Christmas tree still standing in the corner. "If you don't think it's worth donating, we can throw it away."

The sob that escapes Kayla is audible even if she's tried to mask it by putting her hand over her mouth.

"We can do this alone, Lil." Ben wraps his arm around my shoulder. "If there's anything you want to save, you can take it and head back to the city. Kayla and I can handle the rest."

It's a kind offer but judging by the way his arm is shaking, it's a task that is overwhelming to him too. I knew that before we walked through the front door of the house that it would remind him of the day he lost his mother. The city may be different, and the home he lived in then likely doesn't resemble this one at all, but the fact that I lost my mother here reiterates the fact that he lost his mother too.

"Ben is right," Kayla says through a very weak smile. "We can do this, Lil. I think it would be best if you didn't stay."

I want to jump on her words. I don't think anyone knows what is best for me but me. I've learned in therapy that a big part of my journey towards healing is dealing with this house and the overwhelming reminders that hide behind the boarded up windows. My brothers' toys are strewn on the floor near our feet. A row of school pictures is on display on the wall behind Kayla's head. This is where I lived and lost. I have to find the strength to let go if I'm ever going to move on.

"I'll start in here and maybe you can work in the study, Ben." I look at him for reinforcement. "Would it be okay, Kayla, if you packed up the dishes in the kitchen? There are some cardboard boxes in there."

"I can do that." She leans forward, pulling me into a tight hug. "I'll get started now."

I watch her turn to walk quickly through the dining room towards the small kitchen. Her brown hair bouncing from her shoulders as she turns the corner.

"We'll work on this floor first and then we'll talk about the bedrooms." Ben takes a step towards the study. "I can still hire someone to come in and do this."

As strong as the temptation has been to accept that offer, I know that whoever comes in won't take the tender care to pack up my family's things the way I will. I want to honor them and having a stranger thoughtlessly toss their important things into boxes is not the way to do that. "I'll be fine, Ben. Let's get started."

He walks away in silence, scooping up a cardboard box into his palm as he moves past the front door. I'd had the boxes brought in years ago when I felt strong enough to handle the task, but I had scurried back into my pain then. Today was the day that I let my family go.

I busy myself for the next hour, packing away the Christmas tree and all the simple ornaments into boxes labeled for charity. I tenderly wrap all the photos of my siblings and my parents in paper before placing them in a separate box for storage. I handle one piece of my family's history at a time, carefully considering where I want each item to go.

"I need to head back into the city, Lil." Ben calls to me from the doorway of the living room. "One of my patients was just brought in with a serious issue. I need to go."

Even though he'd taken the day off to help me with this, I knew there was a strong possibility that his time would be stolen away. "I'm good here. I can handle the rest of this by myself."

"Kayla can stay." He darts his gaze back to the kitchen. "I can ask her to hang out and help."

I don't know Kayla well enough to ask her to stay with me while I file away my past into labeled boxes and envelopes. "No. You two go now and I'll leave in a couple of hours."

"You're sure?" I can see the relief in his expression. I sensed his concern for her when she broke down into tears earlier. She has no real knowledge of my past. She's only spoken to me a few times. Asking her to stay here alone with me is too much for us both.

"I'd like some time alone here. I need it," I say it with conviction. I do need it.

"Promise me you won't tackle the bedrooms on your own." He leans down to run his hand over the back of my hair. "You and I will come back next week to finish."

I nod in agreement. I can't go upstairs alone. The weight of the night my family died is keeping my feet firmly on the first floor.

Chapter 21

"I know you said I didn't need to come, but I couldn't stay away." Clive's arms are around me the moment I open the door.

"I can't believe you came here." I slide my hands under his suit jacket to embrace him. "I won't ask how you knew the address."

A gentle chuckle races through his body. "It wasn't hard to find."

I nod against his dress shirt. "You should be in the city at your media event."

"It's over." He pulls back slightly so he can gaze down at my face. "It went well. The big announcement was the re-launch of the dating app."

I smile at the grin on his face. "Who do you have working on that?"

"Not you." He runs his index finger over my chin. "It's still going to be a piece of shit, but it will be better than it was."

This is one of those rare moments when I want to ask for my job back. I've held an internal debate almost every day about whether or not I should go back to work for Clive. Our relationship is moving along so effortlessly now, that throwing any curveballs into the mix seems foolish. I want things to stay just as they are. I want to always look into his face and see the affection that is there. "You just need to market it the right way."

"Are you going to offer some free advice?" He whips his smartphone out of the pocket of his suit jacket. "If you are, I'm taking notes."

I glance briefly at his phone. "I'm not offering advice although I could use some."

He steps past me, allowing me to close the door behind him. I watch as he takes in the room and the boxes that spot the floor. "I can hire someone to take care of this for you."

"My friend made the same offer and I told him the same thing I'll tell you," I begin before I stop to look at the now barren fireplace mantle. "It's part of my healing process. I have to do it for my mother and siblings."

"I can understand that." He tucks his hands into the pocket of his pants. "I'm proud of you."

It's the first time he's said it and I'm overwhelmed by the range of feelings it ignites. "You're proud of me?"

"You're so young, Lilly." He takes a step towards me. "I was a mess when I was twenty-two. You're the most graceful, beautiful person I've ever known."

I dip my chin down to shield my expression from his view. I'm touched, deeply touched by his words. "That means a lot to me."

"It's the truth." He pulls in a heavy breath. "You're so strong. I'm in awe of you."

I feel my lip quiver. I don't want to cry. I can't allow this moment to shift into me standing in a puddle of my own tears. "About that advice that I need..."

"The advice," he repeats back as he pushes his feet farther apart. "My advice is to spend more time with your boyfriend."

"Boyfriend?" I parrot the word back with a lift of my brow. "You're my boyfriend now?"

"I've been your boyfriend for weeks now." He leans forward to kiss me gently. "Tell your boyfriend what advice you need."

I try to steel my shaking hands. "I'm going to introduce the organ donation app at our event tomorrow."

I'm surprised by the grin that takes over his mouth. "I'm really happy to hear that, Lilly."

"You are?"

"It's an important development. It's going to help a lot of people."

"So you think it's a good idea?"

"You're doing it under the umbrella of Hughes Enterprises? Alec controls it?" he asks with little inflection in his tone.

"No." I shake my head. "He's letting me present it on my own."

"He is?" This time he can't mask the surprise in his voice.

"I'm presenting one of his apps and then mine."

"You've got him by the balls, don't you?" He skims his hand over my hair.

"Don't talk about Alec's balls."

He closes his eyes briefly before he lets out a roar of laughter. "I won't ever again."

"I'm doing it for them." I nod toward the cardboard box containing my family's photographs. "I made the app for all of them."

"They'd all be very proud of you." His hands jump to my face to cradle it. "I know they would be."

Chapter 22

"Do you think I look nice in this?" I run my hand along the skirt of the dress I've chosen to wear for the event. It's navy blue and the hem falls just below my knee. "I'm really nervous."

"Are you wearing garters?" His hands are on my hips as he whispers the words against my neck. "Tell me what you're wearing under this."

"Mr. Parker." I pull back from his embrace as I see Lance, Alec's assistant, enter the room. "Are you sure it's a good idea for you to be here?"

His eyes dart to where Lance is readying the media packets that will be handed out to everyone in the audience. "Hey, Lance."

"Mr. Parker." Lance doesn't look up from the task he's assigned to do. "Does Mr. Hughes know you're here?"

"I saw Alec on my way in," he says hoarsely. "I'm here to watch Ms. Randall's presentation."

"Sure." Lance scoops up the folders in his hands as he walks back towards the door of the room I've been asked to wait in. "I'll be back to get you in a few minutes, Lilly."

"That gives me enough time to kiss you." His soft lips float over mine before I have a chance to react. I moan into the kiss. I can't curb the desire that overtakes me when I'm this close to him. We'd made love for most of the night at his place after he'd driven me back to Manhattan. He'd held me as I told him stories about each of my siblings. We'd slept no more than an hour but I feel more energized today than I have in a very long time.

"I get hard when you call me Mr. Parker," he whispers the words into my mouth. "You need to do that when I'm inside of you. I want to hear it."

I pull back to look into his eyes. "I thought you wanted me to call you Clive."

"I thought you wanted me to tie you to my bed."

"I'm still waiting for you to do that," I say under a heavy breath. "I want you to control my pleasure."

"I need to be inside of you, Lilly." His hands grab my ass through my dress. "Christ, I need to calm down."

I feel his erection pressed against me. "You can wait here until things settle."

"Lilly, let's go." Lance pokes his head into the doorway. "Alec is getting ready to introduce you now."

"You're going to be amazing." Clive brushes his lips over mine. "I'm so proud of you. I can't tell you how much."

I nod. "You'll be waiting for me when I'm done, right?"

"I'll be in the front row." He pushes my hair from my shoulders. "I'll wait in my seat for you to come to me when you're done."

I give him one last smile before I turn quickly to rush out of the door with Lance hot on my heel.

***

"I think we can all agree that our new shopping app will change the landscape of the gently used clothing market. We've made it faster, easier and more convenient for anyone who wishes to sell last season's wardrobe pieces to make room for this year's stylish new trends," I deliver the words Alec's marketing team had written for me with effortless ease. I've rehearsed the presentation enough times to know exactly what to say and when to say it. I move through the rest of the presentation with a smile on my face and a knot in my stomach.

"The app will be available for download within the next month." I press the remote in my hand to cue up the next slide on the large screen behind me. "We'll have an introductory free trial for ninety days. You can find all the details on our website or within the media packets that are being handed to you now."

I scan the first row of the audience, settling my eyes on Clive's smiling face. This is my moment now. It's when I finally get to share my organ donation app with the world.

"Mr. Hughes has been kind enough to allow me to share an important personal project with all of you today," I hesitate only briefly as I hear a few loud, but indistinguishable voices in the crowd. "I've developed an app that will help millions of people all over the world who are dealing with a very personal and painful situation."

I click the remote in my hand to bring up the first slide in my presentation. It's a simple overview of the app from an aesthetic

140

point of view. "This is something that I've kept close to me for years, but I feel that now is the right time to share it with the world."

An audible gasp fills the room.

I look to the right to see Alec racing across the stage towards me, his face a twisted mix of horror and anger.

My eyes catch the corner of the large screen behind me.

I fall to my knees as I turn to look directly at it.

On full and vivid display is the half-naked picture I sent to Parker.

The same picture Clive tucked into his pocket the first night I met him.

It's the picture he told me he destroyed.

GONE

Part Three

Chapter 1

"Lilly. Please, Lilly, look at me."

It's Clive's voice. I'm crouched into a ball, my arms wrapped around my legs. I press my lips so tightly into my knees that I can't speak. I won't speak. I don't know what I could possibly say to him. He's the one who had my picture in his pocket. He took it and destroyed it. Those are the only words that I can hear reverberating through my mind.

"Someone needs to take that god dammed picture down," Clive yells into the chaos.

There are voices everywhere. I see feet scrambling past me. I can feel hands on my shoulders trying to pull me up but I'm frozen. I can't move. Everything I've worked so hard for has vanished because of that picture.

"Take her out of her now, Alec," Clive seethes.

"What the fuck is going on?" Alec's voice is laced with anger. "Who the hell did this?"

"Lilly," Lance, Alec's assistant, is crouched in front of me. "I need you to come with me now. I can take you to a quiet room. Let me help you get up."

I pull my gaze up to his boyish face. He's not much older than me. The first moment I saw him weeks ago I thought about how he looked like an older version of my brother, Reave. Reave was only ten when he died. I wish he was here. I wish they were all here still. I've tarnished their memories forever now.

"Everyone stays in this room," Clive voice bellows over all the noise. "Sit the fuck down. All of you sit down."

There are muffled shouts thrown back at Clive from the audience of reporters and tech bloggers. I can't clearly make out anything. I feel Lance's hand grab mine and I cling to it. I need his strength to help bring me to my feet.

"If any one of you prints or posts the picture of Ms. Randall, I will personally see to it that your ass is dragged into a costly litigation." The room quiets as Clive continues," I own the copyright to that picture. If you've posted it on any social media sites now is the time to delete it. If you don't, I promise I will hunt you down."

"Lilly." Lance pulls harder on my hand, trying in vain to pull me to my feet. "We need to go. You can't stay here."

"Okay," I agree softly. "I'll go."

I feel weightless as he drops my hand before sliding both of his around my waist. I reach for his shoulders to steady myself. I doubt that my feet will support me so I'm grateful that he's carrying the brunt of my weight.

I don't turn to look at the audience. I can hear my name being tossed out but anything beyond that is unintelligible and lost beneath the low hums of the people standing on the stage. I know they all are thinking the same thing. The reckless abandon of my pose in the picture, and the fact that I had a broad smile on my face as I held open my barista uniform to reveal my nude breasts, draws instant conclusions. They all think I'm a joke. No one in the tech world will ever take me seriously after this.

"We're going down this hallway." Lance gestures with his chin towards a long, narrow hallway that leads back to the room I was in with Clive not more than thirty minutes ago.

I let him lead me all the while trying to keep my head down. I can feel the heated glares of my co-workers from Hughes Enterprises as we walk past them. I've let Alec down. He gave me an incredible opportunity and I not only squandered it away, I damaged the reputation of his company.

"Lilly." As if on cue I hear Alec's deep voice right behind us. Another arm wraps around my waist and I can only assume it's his. "Are you alright?"

I nod knowing that I can't form a concrete response. I'm not alright. I can't wrap my brain around what just transpired on the stage.

"Get her some water," Alec barks at Lance as we round a corner and step into the same room I was in with Clive before I stepped on stage for my presentation. "Lilly, sit down."

I feel him lowering me onto a soft chair. I push my hand back to steady my body not wanting to teeter forward. I'm light headed and weak. I clear my throat softly. "Where's Clive?"

Alec crouches in front of me, pushing a chilled open bottle of water into my palm. "Drink this, Lilly. Take a drink."

I do as I'm told even though I can't tell if I'm thirsty or not. I can't tell anything. "How did that happen?"

"We have no idea." Alec's eyes flit over my face. "Where did that picture come from?"

He deserves an answer. It's his event and my picture has ruined the entire thing for him. Not to mention the lasting damage it's going to do to his business. I haven't worked here a month and already my actions have marred his company's good name forever. "I took that picture. I didn't put it in the slide presentation. I wouldn't do that."

"Shit, Lilly." Alec pushes the bottle of water back towards my lips, encouraging me to take another sip. "You practically fainted out there. I know you had nothing to do with it."

I'm grateful that there's no question in his mind about whether I deliberately tried to sabotage his event. "I'm so sorry."

"Did you have that picture on your computer at the office?" Lance is standing next to me now. "Could someone have accessed it from there?"

I glance up at him and see genuine concern there. We haven't spent a lot of time talking since I began working alongside him, but he's been nothing but kind and welcoming to me. Whenever I've had a question, he's run to find the answer for me. "I took it with a Polaroid camera a few months ago. Clive had it."

Alec scrubs his hand over his forehead. "What do you mean Clive had it?"

I'm not about to launch into the sordid tale of how I met Parker when I was using the dating app developed for Corteck. The details that relate to exactly how the picture ended up in Clive's possession aren't going to change the end result. He's the last person who had that picture. "Clive told me he destroyed the picture weeks ago. That's the last I heard of it."

Alec's eyes dart up from my face towards where Lance is standing behind us. I know what he's thinking. For a fleeting moment of time when I first turned and saw the picture I thought the same thing. Corteck and Hughes Enterprises are direct competitors. They're both fighting to get into the very competitive app market. Sabotaging a press day event would have a lasting impact. I know Clive is ruthless but after all the tender moments we've shared and the words he's whispered into my ear, I can't believe that he'd do something this malicious to me.

"Go get Clive." Alec waves his hand towards the closed door. "Get him the fuck in here now, Lance."

Chapter 2

"Lilly." It's Clive. He's kneeling in front of me now, his hands cradling my face. "Are you okay? You're so pale. Do you need a doctor?"

I do. I wish Ben were here. I've thought about texting him and asking him to come. Right now, he's the only person I can trust. "I'm okay. I don't need a doctor."

"We need to talk, Clive," Alec says. The anger within his tone is clear and palpable. As soon as Lance had left to find Clive, Alec had bolted to his feet and paced the floor in front of me.

"Not now." Clive's eyes don't leave my face. "Who the hell was operating that slide show?"

"Lilly told me you had the picture." I see Alec's finger dart into the air in my peripheral vision. "This is on you, Clive."

Clive's grip on my face tightens. He turns his gaze up towards Alec. I can see the tightness in his jaw as he opens his mouth to speak. "Fuck you. This is all on you. You need to find the asshole that put that picture up."

"How did someone else get the picture?" I whisper the words out not knowing if they're loud enough for Clive to hear. "You had the picture."

His head turns back towards me slowly. "I don't know. I swear I shredded that fucking picture."

I can't pull anything from his stoic expression. I can see concern in his eyes but it's veiled by anger. I watch as he takes a heavy swallow, perspiration building on his upper lip.

He suddenly jerks forward until his lips are hovering next to my ear. "I need you to think very hard about whether you showed that picture to someone other than my brother."

The words sting so deeply that my breathing stalls. I pull back, wanting to look him directly in the eyes when I answer. "Parker was the only one. He was the one I sent it to."

"You're sure?" His brows lift.

I want to wrench free from his grasp but there's no room for me to move. I'm trapped in this chair and in the knowledge that he's questioning a fact that I've been very clear about. He knows that I didn't show that picture to anyone else. "I am positive," I spit the words out clearly, one-by-one.

He rests his forehead against mine. "I have to make a few calls. You stay right here."

I nod even though I know that as soon as I can feel any sensation in my legs again, that I'm going to stand and try to find a back exit so I can slink out of the building. I can't think with everyone milling about me and Clive questioning whether I gave another virtual stranger a peek beneath my barista uniform.

"It's Clive," he snaps into the phone. "I'm sending you a picture. I need copyright on it yesterday. Get your ass to Washington and make it happen now."

My hand fists as I pull myself up. I can't let this happen. It's my picture. I took it. "No, wait."

Clive pulls the phone from his ear. "Lilly, I'm doing this to protect you."

"It's my picture." I briefly glance at Alec and Lance wishing they would leave the room and this conversation. It's too personal. It's all become too personal. "I own the copyright to it. I already do. I know that I do."

A small smile tugs at the edge of his lips. "You do but I'm taking an extra step in case we need to take any action."

My head is still reeling but I'm grounded enough to know that standing in the background while a man like Clive Parker takes ownership over my half-naked picture is not a good idea. We may be connected now but I can't predict the future. I've learned that valuable lesson from my own past. I have to own that picture, and if that means investing every dollar I have to make it happen, I will. "I will handle it myself."

"I have my attorney on the phone right now." He gestures towards his smartphone. "I'll get him to register you as the copyright holder."

That's a debt that I don't want to have hanging over my head. "I have a lawyer. I'll ask him."

I see the doubt in his expression before he even speaks. "My attorney has experience in matters like this. I think you should let me handle it.

I let him walk out of the bistro that night with my picture. I should have kept it when he slid it across the counter to me. I can't make another mistake that will impact my future. I need to take control of this now. "No. I'm going to take care of it."

I watch as his gaze shoots back to where Alec and Lance are standing. I know I'm putting him in a difficult position. He controls every aspect of his life and the lives of those around him and I'm willfully pushing against that. "We'll go to my place and talk about it more, Lilly."

"I can't right now," I say quietly. "I need to talk to Alec."

"Alec?" He sighs. "Why do you need to talk to him?"

I pull on the silver hoop earring dangling from my ear. He's not making this easy for me. "I work for him. I need...I mean, I want to talk to Alec about my future."

His hands leap to my neck, his fingers splaying across my flesh. I flinch when I feel one brush against my scar. "You don't need to do that today. You can come back and work for me."

They were the words that I didn't want to hear. The notion that Clive arranged for that picture to be displayed to hurt me or force me back to Corteck is hovering in the room like a brightly dressed elephant. I know that Alec and Lance have to be thinking the very same thing.

"I'd like to talk to Lil," Alec calls from behind me. "We need to talk."

"Later, Alec," Clive says as he brushes his lips over my forehead. "Give her some time. She's been through enough today."

"She wants to talk to me, Clive." He pushes the point and I'm grateful that he does.

I nod slowly. I need to find out where I stand at Hughes Enterprises. If my ass is going to be tossed into the street, I need to consider what my next move will be. Running back to Clive's company isn't going to happen, especially after what took place today.

"I'm going to go find out who the hell put that picture in the slideshow," he whispers into the skin of my cheek. "Send Lance to find me when you're ready to go home."

I don't respond. I can't. I just stare into the face of the man I thought was my saving grace. Now, all I see is someone I'm not sure I can trust.

Chapter 3

"You need to go home to rest, Lilly. Take the weekend to yourself and if you still need more time, it's yours, with pay."

"I can quit, Alec."

He rests his hands on my shoulders. "You're not quitting."

"You can fire me. You have every reason to."

"I'd be an idiot to fire you." He chuckles softly. "Shit happens. We're going to help you get through this."

The words buoy my sprits enough that I feel part of the weight I've been carrying the past hour lifted from my shoulders. "I'm still not sure how this happened."

"Did you put together the slideshow yourself or did someone help you?" Lance asks from where's he's been seated on a chair by the door. He saw Clive out and then shut the door with an unceremonious thud the moment he left the room. It's obvious that Lance believes Clive is involved in what happened today.

"I put it together." I cross my arms over my chest. "I saved it on a flash drive that I gave to Cheryl from communications. She was handling all the media stuff."

"Cheryl?" Alec glances past me to Lance. "Who is that?"

"Cheryl's worked here for eight months." Lance scrolls over the tablet in his hand. "I've got her personnel file here if you want a look."

Alec motions with his right hand. "Give it to me."

I stand in silence as I watch him scan the screen. "She's a grandmother. Why would she put up that picture?"

Lance reaches to grab the edge of the tablet. "I can run a more extensive background check on her if you want."

"I want you to go find her now."

"I've got it," Lance says excitedly. "Should I take someone to back me up?"

"Back you up?" Alec cocks a dark brow with the question. "What the fuck does that mean?"

"What if she won't cooperate with me?" Lance spits the words out quickly. "I mean…what if she realizes that we're on to her."

"Christ, Lance." Alec points directly at the door. "If you can't handle a sixty-year-old grandmother, you're fired."

I feel a surge of laughter at the words. I pull my hand to my lips to try to contain the urge to chuckle.

Alec stares down at me as we both hear the door close behind Lance. "This isn't the end of the world, Lil. We'll take care of whoever did this to you. You can count on that."

***

"Did you get an offer on the house?" Garrett Ryan, the attorney that has been helping me for the past few years asks.

"No." I smooth my hands over the denim of the jeans I'm wearing. After Lance drove me home, I'd changed quickly and hopped into a taxi with the hope that Garrett would be able to squeeze in a moment with me before he took off the for weekend. He's one of the best probate attorneys in all of Manhattan and getting in to see him typically takes weeks.

"My assistant told me that you said it was urgent when you arrived."

I take a deep breath. "I'm in trouble, Garrett."

"What kind of trouble?" He glances at my face, his eyes locking on mine. "What's happened?"

Ever since Garrett became my legal counsel when I turned eighteen, our correspondence has been mainly limited to the occasional email or phone call about my grandmother's estate, my parent's house and the life insurance proceeds from my mother's policy. I've never touched the money. I can't bring myself to do anything with it knowing that it's the result of my father's unrestricted rage.

"Were you arrested?"

I smile knowing that it's likely one of the first questions when a client shows up unannounced in a panic at their lawyer's office. I'm tempted to ask what he thinks I'd be arrested for but I'm here for one reason and one reason only. "No, it's nothing like that."

"Tell me what it is, Lilly." He grins at me. "The first step is the hardest. You need to confess if I'm going to help you with anything."

I soak in his features. I've always thought he was very handsome. I felt a misplaced emotional connection to him after my grandmother died and he took time out of his life to help me pack up her things. It was a kind gesture that I absorbed as more than that. He set me straight by explaining how much he cared for the woman he was dating at the time. He let me down, effortlessly and easily, even though I never revealed that I was crazy about him.

"I can start guessing if you want?" He sits up straighter. "Do you have a bunch of unpaid traffic tickets?"

"I don't own a car, Garrett."

"Did you steal a chocolate bar from the bodega by your place?"

I can't contain a small smile. "I'm trying to eat less sugar."

"You didn't punch someone on the subway, did you?" His gaze slides over my face. "We won't have a case unless he was feeling you up."

"I want to punch someone," I mutter under my breath.

"Who?" He tilts his chin up. "Did someone do something to you?"

I have to tell him. I got in the taxi with every intention of being mature and professional about this. It's just a picture. I need to just spit the words out so he can tell me what my next step should be. "I…there's a picture of me…I'm naked and…"

I'm so startled by the sudden ringing of my smartphone that it falls from my palm onto the carpeted floor of his office. I reach down, fumbling for it, all the while aware that I just confessed to there being a nude photo of me in existence.

"Do you need to get that?" He's on his feet now, peering over his desk to where I'm on my hands and knees on the floor.

I hit the mute button after I see Clive's name flash across the screen. I look up into Garrett's face. "No. I need you to help me. I've ruined my life."

Chapter 4

"I'm going to need to see that picture, Lilly," Garrett says as he helps me back into the chair in front of his desk.

"Why?" I push my phone into my purse. "I told you that I was nude. Don't you believe me?"

"I believe you. I just need to know what we're dealing with." He sits down in the chair next to me. "Tell me about the picture. Did someone post it online?"

"I'm not sure," I answer honestly.

"You're not sure?" He clears his throat. "I'm your attorney. You don't need to be embarrassed. I can help but only if I have a clear understanding of what's going on."

I'm telling myself that he's right. My mind knows it but the knot that has formed in the pit of my stomach isn't agreeing with that. "I'll start at the beginning."

"It's a good place." He pats his hand over my knee.

I lean back in the chair hopeful that the slight bit of physical distance I've created between us will help me feel less exposed. "I met a guy named Parker when I was testing out a dating app. That was months ago."

"Did you send him a picture over the app?"

I reach for my neck, my fingers searching in vain for the necklace my mother gave to me on my fourteenth birthday. "The app didn't work so we started emailing."

"You emailed the picture then?" His tone is patient and soft even though it's almost six o'clock and his day should be done by now.

"No, I snail mailed it. He asked me to send him a Polaroid picture." I drop my hands to my lap. "I did that. I sent some other things with the picture."

"What other things?" He leans back in the chair, crossing his legs. "Did you send more than one picture?"

"Just the one." My index finger darts into the air. "I sent a letter and the panties that I was wearing in the picture."

"So you weren't completely nude in the photograph?"

My hand leaps to my chest. "My breasts…they show in the picture. I'm wearing panties though."

"You sent the picture to this guy Parker." He drums his fingers against his thigh. "What did he do with the picture?"

"Nothing," I say. "He actually gave me his brother's address so I mailed the picture and other stuff there."

"What's his brother's name?"

"Clive Parker," I blurt out without hesitation. "Clive Parker is the one who had my picture."

***

"Sorry about that, Lilly." He places his smartphone on his desk. "I was supposed to meet my buddy, Nathan, for a drink. He's in town from Boston."

"We can do this another time," I lie. I want to do it now. I've confessed so much already that I'm worried that if we agree to meet on Monday that I'll retreat into a cocoon and hide away forever.

His brows rise. "I know it's not easy to talk about this. I'll see Nate tomorrow. This is more important."

I'm grateful that he understands the urgency that I'm feeling. I've heard the muffled rumbles of my phone ringing from inside my closed purse. I know, without question, that it's Clive. I have to understand my legal options before I talk to him again. I owe that to myself. "I really appreciate you taking out this much time for me."

"You said that Clive Parker had the picture?" His brows rise. "You don't mean the Clive Parker that owns that tech company, do you?"

I stare down at my fingernails. I've come this far and leaving out any relevant details isn't going to change what happened earlier. "Yes, I mean him."

"You sent a Polaroid picture of your exposed breasts to Clive Parker?"

"Yes," I answer wearily. "I didn't know it was his address. The Parker I was emailing with is Clive Parker's half-brother."

He traces a path over his left eyebrow with his fingers. I can tell that he's trying to absorb everything that I'm telling him. "So Clive Parker has that picture?"

I scrub my hand over the back of my neck. "He did. He told me he destroyed it but I don't know if he has."

"He's a high profile businessman," he says curtly. "Is there a reason you don't believe him?"

There shouldn't be. I shouldn't have to question anything that Clive has told me after what we've shared together but I can't deny what I saw with my own two eyes. "I had to give a presentation at work today…"

"Where are you working now?" he asks, seeming genuinely interested. "When you emailed me about selling your folks' house, you mentioned getting a job but you didn't say where."

I can skip the part about working at Corteck for a hot minute because it's not relevant. "I'm working for Hughes Enterprises."

"Impressive." He kicks his foot out to tap my leg softly. "You put other kids your age to shame."

I smile at the suggestion than I'm a kid. I searched online for any tidbits I could pull up about Garrett before I took the train from Boston to New York to meet him the first time. He's younger than Clive and the fact that he views me as a child makes me instantly aware that Clive may see me as naïve and easily fooled. "I've worked really hard to get to the place I am."

"What happened at work today?" he presses on.

"I was giving a presentation at a media event. I had to introduce two new apps. One was developed at Hughes and the…" my voice trails when I realize I'm rambling. "None of this matters."

"It all matters," he says patiently. "Did something happen with the picture at work?"

I swallow past the growing lump in my throat. "There was a slideshow."

"Lilly?" He taps my leg with his hand. "Tell me."

I pull all the courage I can find into the next breath I take. "I was talking and then I turned around and the picture of me… that picture was on the screen."

Chapter 5

I walk back into his office after spending the past five minutes in the restroom splashing cool water on my face. Telling Garrett about the picture wasn't easy but it was necessary. I feel a small sense of relief knowing that I'm doing what I need to do to protect my reputation.

"I'll talk to Alec Hughes," Garrett pauses as he looks down at his smartphone. "Do you think he'd be available to talk to me tonight?"

"I think so," I offer. "It happened at his company's event."

"You're okay to get home on your own?" He motions towards the door of his office.

"I am." I'm surprised that my voice sounds as calm as it does. I've been dreading this moment since I left my apartment earlier. I know Clive will be waiting for me there.

"Can I get Parker's email address before you leave?" He doesn't bring his gaze up from his phone's screen. "Or do you have his number?"

"Parker's in Dubai." I tilt my head to the side. "Clive sent him there a few weeks ago on some work project."

"Did you have a personal relationship with Parker?" He looks directly at me. "I mean, was there ever anything between you two beyond the picture and emailing?"

"No." I shake my head violently from side-to-side. "I only met Parker in person once. It was at the bistro."

"He came to see you at work?"

I had one foot out the door and now I'm being pulled back into the pit of my mistakes. "He was there. Clive called him down there."

"Clive Parker was at the bistro?" He exhales audibly. "You've known him since then?"

"I met him at the bistro." I roll my shoulders back to try and get more air into my lungs. I feel out of breath.

"Have you seen him since then?" His voice is husky. "Have you seen him since you moved to New York?"

"Yes," I whisper. "I've seen him here."

"I'm missing something." He crosses his arms over his chest. "Fill in the blanks."

I want to but revealing my intimate relationship with Clive isn't something I thought I'd have to do. I'm not ashamed of it. The gnawing ache in the back of my mind that's telling me that Clive has been manipulating me this entire time won't stop. It's only becoming stronger and stronger the more I try and ignore it. "The blanks?"

"Lilly," he says my name slowly. "I'm a lawyer. I can tell when people are withholding. I'll help you but you need to be honest. I can ask you or I can ask Alec Hughes."

Shit. He's one hundred percent right. Alec will tell him that I'm dating Clive.

"I've been sleeping with Clive Parker." My eyes plead with his. I don't want his mouth to fall open or for him to launch into a lecture about how Clive is too old for me and I should be dating someone my own age.

I see his jaw flinch slightly but anything other than that is masked behind his experience as an attorney. "Is it serious or more of a casual thing?"

I'm tempted to ask if this particular line of questioning is relevant to my nude picture or not, but I opt for the honest answer. "I don't know."

"You don't know?"

Any semblance of trying to appear to be a mature adult who is complete control of her life just flew out the window. "I thought it was serious but I'm not sure after what happened today."

He runs his hand over his chin. "You said earlier that Clive was the last person to have the picture of you?"

"Yes." I tip my chin forward. "He told me he destroyed it."

"But you saw it today?"

"Everyone saw it today," I mutter under my breath.

His eyes rest on my face. "This isn't my area of expertise, Lilly. I don't think we need to file a copyright notice. I'm certain you already own it. I'm going to consult with a colleague on your legal rights regarding the picture, but…"

"Thank you," I interrupt knowing that what he was about to say isn't something I'm certain I can do.

"Stay away from him for the time being." He rests his hand on my elbow. "Until we have a better understanding of what happened and who is behind it, I'd strongly advise you to steer clear of Clive Parker."

Chapter 6

"You can't do that to me." Clive pulls me into his chest the moment I step out of the taxi in front of my building. "Where have you been? Why haven't you answered your phone?"

They're the expected questions that a man asks a woman he cares for when she disappears after a traumatic event. I should find comfort in them and in the way he's clinging to me, but I can't. All I can see is him back at the bistro, shoving my picture into his pocket. "I went to see my attorney."

"What's his name?" he asks into my hair. "I'd like to speak with him."

"Have you been waiting long?" I'm not asking because I'm concerned about how he's wasted his time standing on the street in front of my building. I don't want him to talk to Garrett. I need to gain perspective and find my own path out of this nightmare and I can't do that if he's influencing the only person who is looking out for my legal best interests. I have no doubt that if I tell Clive that my attorney is named Garrett Ryan that he'll call him up immediately and tell him that I no longer need his services.

His head dips down to his wristwatch. "I've been here for more than an hour."

"It's been a really hard day." I look at the sidewalk. "I think I'm just going to go up to my place and sleep."

"No." His arm slides from my back to my waist. "I'll come up with you and we'll talk."

I run both of my hands over my forehead. "I don't feel talking right now, Clive."

"Lilly." He pulls back. "Look at me."

I need to. I don't see how I'm going to be able to end this conversation without looking at him. I casually drift my eyes over his face before settling them on a spot just past his right ear. "I'd like to go up to my apartment."

I flinch when I feel his strong hand grab my chin. "Look me in the eye."

I trace the fingers of my left hand over my lips, trying to gather the strength to face him directly. I need to shield all of the doubt I'm feeling. If I don't, this evening will never end. "What is it?"

In the dim light that the streetlights cast down on us, he studies my face. "You look exhausted."

I feel my bottom lip quiver so I race my tongue over it, hoping to quiet it. "I can't think straight at this point. Sleep will help."

"I can stay with you." He tilts his chin towards the front door of my building. "Or we can go to my place if you'd be more comfortable there."

He wants to pull me back into the comfort of his bed. He'll kiss me, touch me and chase away all the lingering doubts. "I think I'll just stay here by myself tonight."

"I don't think that's a good idea," he presses as he begins to steer me towards the front door. "I'll just stay until you fall asleep."

My avenue of escape is narrowing. I have to do something if I want the space and peace I need to think about today. "Did you find out who put the picture in the slideshow?"

His feet stop in place just as his hand drops from the small of my back. "Not yet."

"Alec was going to talk to the woman who I gave the flash drive with my slides to." I look up and into his face. "Do you know if he talked to her?"

He looks past me towards the softly lit foyer of my building. "I believe he did, yes."

"What did she say?" I push not only because I want to know if Cheryl has any knowledge of what happened but because I want to gauge Clive's reactions.

"She's as stumped as the rest of us."

I keep my eyes focused on him even though he won't look at me. "How can that be?"

"You're tired, Lilly." He leans forward to brush his lips against my forehead. "I think sleep is probably the best thing for you. I'll call you in the morning."

I close my eyes just as he turns and walks away.

Chapter 7

My initial plan when I was eating ice cream and watching a movie at midnight was to bury my phone at the bottom of my clothes hamper, ignore the buzzer to my apartment and spend the entire weekend wrapped up in my own thoughts. That lasted until ten this morning when Ben called me three times in a row. I ignored the first two calls but when I saw his number flash across the screen for a third time within five minutes, panic set in. I answered immediately.

Now, three hours later I'm sitting at a table in Axel NY staring at him and Kayla. They can't stop smiling and the fact that I feel like shit and likely look like hell isn't registering with either of them. "What's going on?" I ask tentatively.

"We didn't just call you down here to have lunch," Ben says loudly. "I mean we love spending time with you, Lil, but we have something to tell you."

It has to be good news. Judging by the way he keeps kissing her cheek I'd bet money that they're not breaking up. They're engaged so it's either a wedding date or…

"We're having a baby," Kayla blurts out. "Ben and I are having a baby."

My eyes volley from her face back to his. I want to cry, not because I'm so thrilled for the two of them. I am. I know Ben will be an amazing father and his child will never want for anything. I want to cry because this is what it looks like when two people who love each other start a family. This is the joy that is in their faces. The last time I sat at a table and was told a baby was on the way was much different than this. My mother was shedding tears of sorrow over the fact that she was pregnant with my youngest brother, River. He only lived to be five-years-old.

"Did you hear her, Lil?" Ben is almost bouncing out of his chair. "We're going to have a baby."

My hand leaps to my mouth. I push against my lips to hold in a sob. "I'm so happy for you both," I whisper between my fingers.

"I'm having the waiter bring over some champagne for Ben and your friend." A deep voice from the right invades our conversation. "Do you want some sparkling juice or water, Kayla? I can see if we have any non-alcoholic champagne."

"Thank you, Hunter." Kayla reaches to touch the top of his hand. "Juice would be good."

Hunter. I know who he is. He's the man who is raising Clive's nephew, Cory.

"I'm sorry, Hunter." Kayla chuckles softly. "This is our friend, Lilly."

He reaches his hand to me and I grab onto it without hesitation. This is the only person, besides Parker, who is part of Clive's family. I stare at him, taking in the kindness of his smile as he stares down at me. "It's my pleasure, Lilly."

"How do you know Ben?" I ask without thinking. Judging by the fact that Ben has already invited me to Axel NY twice, I'm guessing that he's a regular.

"I'm friends with Hunter's wife," Kayla explains. "We've been friends since college."

The world is a very small and random place. "That's amazing. I've heard great things about Sadie."

All three sets of eyes hone in on me. I said it without thinking and now I'm going to have to explain not only how I know Sadie's name but also, who has told me about her.

"Wait." Hunter takes a full step back just as his hand flies to his chin. "I know you."

He doesn't. I've never met the man. He's thinking of some other redhead who knows his wife. I don't even technically know her. I only know of her because of my Clive Parker fact finding missions online and the few small details he offered about her. "We've never met."

"You're dating Clive." A small grin pulls at the corner of his mouth. "You're that Lilly."

"You're dating Clive Parker?" Kayla's hand falls to the table with a dull, empty thud. "Why didn't you tell me you were dating Clive Parker?"

Why can't I rewind time to the moment when Hunter walks over to our table, so can I duck underneath it?

"It's really new and we haven't discussed whether…"

"I used to date his brother, Parker."

"What?" I spit the word out with more distaste than I intend. "You dated Parker?"

"Have you met him?" She leans both elbows on the table. "I haven't seen him in months."

I stare at Ben. He's listening intently to Kayla, with a broad smile on his face. I, on the other hand, feel as though I'm about to scream. How is it even remotely possible that my only friend's fiancée used to date my boyfriend's brother?

"Lilly?" She taps her fingers over my hand. "Have you met Parker?"

"Once." I look up at Hunter's face. He seems just as invested in this conversation as Kayla is. "He came to the bistro I was working at one night so it was a quick hello. That's it."

"That's so random." She throws her head back in gleeful laughter. "I can't believe you're dating Clive."

I can't believe Hunter knows I'm dating Clive. I came to this lunch hoping that a few hours with Ben and Kayla would help boost my spirits and take my mind off of what happened yesterday. Now, I've been forced to reveal that I'm dating a man I'm not sure I want to even see again.

"Don't tell Clive this but years ago I signed up to get news alerts whenever his name popped up." Hunter's body shakes with a deep laugh. "I don't check it all the time but last week I clicked on a link and there was your face."

He said last week so that rules out last night. Gauging by the way he's not judging me, I'm going to guess that he doesn't know that my breasts were the stars of the tech show that Hughes Enterprises put on yesterday. "My face popped up?"

"It was an image of you and Clive at a restaurant." He pulls his face into a mock scowl. "It wasn't one of my restaurants though."

"I had no idea." I don't take my eyes off of him. "I'll have to look that up."

"I'll find it right now." He fishes his smartphone out of the pocket of his black pants. "I'll just search your name."

"No," I practically scream the word. "I'd rather we toast to Ben and Kayla's new baby."

"Right." Hunter snaps his fingers. "I'll go get the champagne and juice and we'll celebrate."

I heave a sigh at the reprieve. I have no doubt that if Hunter Reynolds would have searched my name that he'd get an eyeful of me I never want him to see.

Chapter 8

I've searched my name online three times since I came home from the restaurant and the only reference to what happened yesterday is a brief mention of the picture at the end of a blogger's comments about the shopping app. The picture didn't pop up at all but it's only been a day and the search engine's algorithms may need some time to catch up. I'm going to enjoy the calm before the storm and ready myself for what my uncertain future holds. I need to focus on showing Alec that he made the right decision in keeping me on at Hughes Enterprises, I need to find out from Garrett what I can do to protect my rights and I have to find out who set me up.

I hear the faint knock at my door just as the sound of heavy footsteps stop. Anyone who walks into the foyer who doesn't live here is supposed to buzz the apartment they want to visit, but it's a futile idea. The latch on the inner door of the lobby is loose so virtually anyone can wander in and out freely. I've been meaning to bring it up to with the super but my breast scandal has cleared my mind of every other thought.

I pull open the door even though I know who is standing on the other side of it. He's texted me twice already today. I told him that I was meeting friends for lunch and then had to catch up on some work but the man either can't read between the lines of a subtle hint or he refuses to align himself with anyone's needs but his own in the moment. I told him I'd talk to him on Monday. It's Saturday afternoon and I need to face him and this.

"Do you want to come in or should we go across to the coffee shop to talk?" I motion towards my still barren living room.

"I'd like to be alone with you." He leans against the door. "We need to talk, Lilly."

"We do," I agree. "There's no place here to talk comfortably."

"The coffee shop is too loud." He taps his shoe on the floor. "I'd like to take you back to my condo."

The suggestion that more will happen than a conversation is right there in the air between us. He wants me and even if I couldn't see the evidence of that in his eyes, I'd know it from the tone of his voice.

He reaches to touch my hand. "We can just talk if you want."

Even when I'm trying to block out every emotion that I'm feeling, he can still read my mind. "I just want to talk."

"That's exactly what we're going to do then."

I hesitate for only a brief moment. I want to rid myself of the cloak of doubt that is weighing me down. I want to breathe again and I can't do that until he tells me how my picture ended up on that screen. "I'll get my purse and my keys."

***

"You were shivering in the taxi on the way here." He wraps his arm around my shoulders. "Why don't you sit down? I'll make you some tea."

It's too kind of a gesture for the moment. I'm shivering because I'm a jumble of nerves. He spent the entire ride over talking on his phone to his assistant, Bruce. Clive doesn't stop working, even on the weekends and judging by the single side of the conversation I was privy to, he'll be spending much of tomorrow in his office in meetings with associates from Europe.

"I don't want anything." I pull away from him and move towards an arm chair. "I'd like to talk about yesterday."

He rubs his hand over the front of his neck before he nods. "I know you're devastated over what happened, Lilly."

The words hold more meaning than the delivery he provides. He's very calm and in control. I want him to be as torn up over what happened to me as I am but I've learned over the years of being on my own that we all have to own our emotions. We can't look to others for compassion or sympathy. I'm looking at him right now and all I see is a man with a rehearsed answer for any question I'm about to ask.

"You were the last person to have that picture, Clive." Easing into this with pleasantries and small talk isn't going to help me find the truth about what happened. I want answers. I need them and now that I'm in his condo, I'm not planning on leaving until I have them.

He walks towards where I'm sitting and for a very brief moment I wonder if he's going to drop to his knees and kiss me. My resolve is strong but when he's so close to me, the want is right there, rounding the corner and almost overtaking my willpower to resist him.

He sits on the edge of the table near me. I tuck my legs up, not wanting him to touch me. The motion doesn't go unnoticed. He stares at my jeans briefly before he pulls his darkened gaze to my face. "Ask me already, Lilly. Just ask."

I look down at his hands. They're knotted together in a twisted mess. He's cracking his knuckles and snaking the fingers of his left hand with the right. His anxiety is as evident as mine. I see it now.

"Ask you what?" I push back not wanting to be put on the spot.

"You know what." He leans back to rest one hand against the glass of the table. "Just ask."

Once I toss the question out there the entire dynamic of our relationship will shift. I'll be the accuser and if he had nothing to do with the picture being displayed, I'll have to live with the regret of doubting his word. I scratch the back of my head, trying to figure out a way out. I want the things he said to me while we stood in the living room of my parent's home to be real. I want to believe that the adoration I feel in his kiss is sincere. I want that. I don't want to lose it.

"I am crazy about you, Lilly." He swallows so hard I can hear it. "I am so fucking crazy about you."

I cast my gaze down so I can focus my thoughts. I run my hand along the arm of the chair. "I know that you care about me."

"It's so much more than that." The soft rasp in his voice is disarming. "I love being around you. I never smiled before I met you. I never wanted to smile.

They are beautiful and thoughtful words that I would have fallen into two days ago. Now, I know that the truth is buried somewhere within them. If he didn't have anything to do with the picture being broadcast for the entire room to see, he would have said as much. He would have just come out and told me.

"You and Parker are the only two people who saw that picture." I point my finger at him. "I want to know how it happened. I want you to tell me, Clive."

His head drops to his hands. "Someone else saw the picture. I believe someone else has a copy and it's my fault."

Chapter 9

"Who?" My legs dart out so quickly that my feet smash into the edge of the table. "Who has a copy?"

"Shit, Lilly." He reaches for my foot. "You slammed that into the table. Let me have a look."

The pain that is rushing through me from my stubbed toe is only quieted by my incessant need to know who he showed me picture to. "You showed me picture to someone? Who?"

"I didn't show it to her by choice," he says the words so quickly that they meld into one another.

"Her?" I spit the word at him. "A woman saw it?"

I'm not sure why it's as surprising as it is. I don't really know Clive Parker that well and I've based my assumption that he's only been dating me on his words and the tender way he brings me pleasure in bed. I have no idea if he's been sharing details of our trysts with another woman or not. I didn't bother to ask because I was too busy coming under his tongue.

I'm an idiot sometimes. I may have an honor's degree from MIT but I'm not the brightest bulb when it comes to men. The fact that I sent a nude photo of myself to a strange man is proof enough of that.

"It was that first night in Boston," he says quietly. "The night I came to the bistro."

I nod. I'll never forget that night for a million different reasons. "I remember."

"I was there to see Cory for the weekend," he stops to take a breath. "I was dating a woman at the time so I took her with me."

I recall him saying something to Parker that night about a woman. I hadn't paid any mind to the details of their conversation. Back then, I thought the worst part of my naked picture nightmare was Parker's brother seeing it by mistake. "She's the one who has a copy?"

"I think so." He bends forward, pulling my foot into his lap. "I'm worried that you broke your toe. You hit it so hard."

I can't tell if it's a ploy to steer our conversation off track or not. I'm not going to waste any time trying to figure that out. I swat his hand away softly. "It's fine. Please tell me more about that woman."

"I was on the phone when we walked into the condo and she went into the office to turn on the computer so she could print out a document she was emailed."

"You were angry with Parker for leaving the envelope on your desk."

He had scolded Parker in front of me for that. I can't remember the exact words he said to him but the condensed version was that Clive wasn't going to get laid because his date found the envelope with my picture and the letter.

"She saw it and threw it all at me." He shakes his head. "We weren't that serious. It was mostly friendly fuck..."

I wince at the words. The evidence of his many lovers is online in the form of pictures of him at events and dinners with different women. We haven't talked about it at any length because I don't want to know the details. I'm not a jealous person but the idea of Clive in bed with anyone else, makes me feel raw inside.

"I'm sorry." He rests his hand on the arm of the chair I'm sitting in. "It was nothing like what we have."

I'm not sure what we have so I'm not the best gauge to measure by. "You don't need to be sorry. I had lovers before I met you."

He closes his eyes tightly. "I don't want to know about that."

"Have you talked to her about the picture?" I ask because I don't want to know any details about what happened between the two of them that night or any other night.

"I called her today." He rubs his hand over the soft hair covering his chin. "We're going to meet to talk about it."

Call me foolish but planning a meeting around someone's naked picture seems excessive. "Why didn't you just ask her about it on the phone, Clive?"

"I did."

He doesn't offer more even though I wait with expectation in my eyes. "What did she say?"

"She wants to see me." He deliberately avoids looking at me. "I can read her better in person. I can get the truth out of her."

I stare at the side of his face as he surveys the large windows that overlook the skyline of Manhattan. "I feel as though I'm dangling by a thread."

His eyes dart back to me. "I know, Lilly."

"You don't know." I push against the chair's arm, trying to pull myself up. "You just don't know."

"I'm trying my best to get to the bottom of this for you." He's on his feet. His hand outstretched towards me. "I know how to handle this."

As much as I want to laugh at his words, I can't. "Tell me her name, Clive."

"Let me talk to her first, Lilly."

"I want to know her name."

"I can't be sure if it was her or Parker." His shoulders slump forward. "I have someone in Dubai going through Parker's phone to see if he captured an image of that picture of you."

"Parker has no reason to hurt me," I say the words as if I mean them. I was nothing but a brief Internet fling to Parker. He hasn't emailed me since that night so I have no idea if he'd do anything to jeopardize my career or not. There is no logical reason for him to go to the trouble of sabotaging my presentation.

"I still think it's worthwhile to check his phone."

I finally stand, suddenly feeling a renewed sense of energy. "Why won't you tell me her name?"

"I told you," he begins before he reaches to grab my hand. "I have to be certain first. If it was her, I'll take care of it."

I pull my hand from his. "You're choosing her over me."

His brows pop up. "That's ridiculous."

I try to step past him but the path between the table and the chair is too narrow for us both. "I have a right to know her name."

"As soon as I speak with her, I'll call you."

It's futile. I can stand here, in front of him and demand an answer but it's glaringly obvious that he's not going to give it to me. He promised me he'd protect me and the first time he has an opportunity to do it, he chooses to leave me flailing in an emotional windstorm.

I pull back when he moves to kiss me goodbye. I grab my purse, march towards the door and leave him and his secret lover's name behind.

Chapter 10

"I haven't seen that picture of Parker before." The security guard at Corteck leans over his small desk. "It's a good one."

It's not. It's the picture Parker emailed me when we first started communicating. Correction. It's the first picture of his face that Parker emailed me. He thought it was proper form to send me a picture of his dick first. Good manners do not rampant in that family.

"I like it." I try to sound as though I'm swooning as I tuck my tablet back into my purse. "I think he looks hot in it."

The elderly man laughs so raucously that his head falls back. "You kids and your funny phrases."

Hear that? That's the sound of me getting exactly what I want.

I flirted with him when I first walked into the lobby five minutes ago. Then I told him I was crazy about Parker and now that I've backed it up with proof, the man is putty in my hands.

"Did you know that Mr. Parker sent Parker to Dubai?" I push my bottom lip out for added emphasis. "I miss my little pumpkin so much."

Eww. I'm going to need a shower after this conversation.

"I bet he misses you more." His eyes travel down to my cleavage. Digging the one push-up bra I own out of the bottom of my drawer had been the easy part. Trying to get used to the under wires that are practically stabbing my sides is another thing. I take a deep breath, reminding myself why I'm here in the first place.

"I cried last night because…" I whimper softly as I lean over his desk. "I lost my phone last night so I can't call Parker since I didn't memorize his new number."

"You poor thing." He touches the top of my hand. "You know Mr. Parker isn't in today, right? He doesn't work on Sundays."

I know, from overhearing Clive's conversation in the taxi yesterday, that he's going to be in within the next couple of hours. That's the only reason I'm doing this, right now, at the crack of dawn. "I don't think I can wait until tomorrow to get Parker's number. Can you call Mr. Parker and ask him for it?"

His lips pull back in shock. You'd think I'd asked the man in uniform for his social security number. "Mr. Parker doesn't like to be disturbed unless it's an emergency."

I was counting on that. "I get it."

"If you come back tomorrow, the receptionist who sits over there can help you out." He points towards the main desk in the lobby. If he's referring to the woman who is usually here during the week, she's not willing to help anyone out.

"Can I just wait here until then?" I ask even though I know how ridiculous it sounds. Parker isn't worth losing any sleep over and he sure as hell isn't worth wasting an entire day on. "I can't think or sleep if I can't talk to my precious Parker."

His eyes lock on mine. I have to keep it together if I want him to buy what I'm selling. I rub the end of my nose as I manage to pull out a little sob from within.

"I shouldn't do this." His eyes slide up to the security cameras that dot the ceiling. "I think I can pull up Parker's number on my computer if he's working for the company in Dubai."

I know that he can. That's the entire reason I dragged myself out of bed and put on all this make-up. "Are you serious? You would do that for me?"

"There's nothing like young love." He taps a few keys on his computer with his index finger. "It'll take me a few minutes but I'll find it."

It would take me all of ten seconds to find it, but I just stand there smiling at him, knowing that I got exactly what I came here for.

Chapter 11

"Lilly?" Parker's voice sounds exactly as I remember it. "The Lilly from the coffee shop?"

Considering I was wearing my bistro uniform when I took my now infamous nudie shot, I may need to get used to being known simply as 'Lilly from the coffee shop.' I find a small amount of comfort in the fact that Parker doesn't know my last name. "Yes, that Lilly," I say into my smartphone.

I wait with baited breath to see whether he's going to ask how I got his number. I have a lame excuse at the ready about asking for it at the automotive parts store he worked at in Boston. I'm not even sure anyone there cared enough about him to ask for it. I'm guessing that the fact that I bothered to call him at all will catch him so off guard that he'll skip right over that issue.

"Hey." I hear an edge of excitement in his voice. "What's going on with you?"

I breathe a sigh of relief.

You have no idea, Parker. Seriously. No idea at all.

"Not a lot," I lie. "How are things in Dubai?"

I can hear the muted sounds of voices in the background. It's evening there so he has to be out on the town. "It's okay. I don't know a lot of people here."

"Hey, I've got a small world story for you." I've debated using this as a means to gain Parker's trust but if I want to find out who the mysterious woman is that Clive is protecting, I need to use every available resource I have.

"Really?" I can hear the hesitation in his voice even though he's half a world away. "What do you mean?"

"My best friend is engaged to your ex."

"What ex?"

I make a mental note to leave that out of this story if I ever retell it to Kayla.   "Kayla."

"Kay?"

"I met her a few weeks ago," I offer. "I just realized the other day that you're her ex."

"That's crazy." He chuckles softly. "You seriously know Kayla?"

"It's nutty, right?" I try to control the building anxiety in my voice. "It's that whole six degrees of separation thing."

"How is she?" he asks without any hesitation. "You said she's getting married?"

"She's good." I don't offer any details about her pregnancy because that's not his business. I'm already overstepping a boundary by telling him that she's getting married.

"Is she marrying the doctor?"

I'm mildly surprised that he knows about Ben. I've never heard Ben mention Kayla's ex-boyfriend, which isn't a shock. Ben's so wrapped up in his love for her that I doubt he thinks about her past or his much at all anymore. "That's the guy. They're stoked about getting married."

"I'm happy for her." I can hear the smile in the tone of his voice. "You can tell her that for me."

I can but I won't. In anyone else's eyes I don't have a logical reason for calling Parker on the phone. I shouldn't be talking to him at all, but he can answer the one question that Clive won't. I'm going to lead Parker right down a path towards telling me the name of the woman who was with Clive in Boston.

***

"Is Mrs. Mitchell in today?" I ask the middle- aged woman adjusting the painting on the wall of the gallery.

She turns quickly and gives me the once over. "Who are you?"

I didn't want to give Clive's ex-lover a heads-up. I'd actually waited on a park bench across the street for an hour hoping to catch her before she arrived at work. I'd finally given up after calling Alec and telling him that I'd be taking him up on his offer for an extra day off. It is ten now on Monday morning and I've been rehearsing for the better part of a day what I'll say to the woman who was with Clive that night.

"I asked for your name." She sighs heavily. "Do you have an appointment?"

174

I resort to my trusty trick of only answering the last question when asked more than one. "I didn't know I needed one. I'm new to the city."

Her face softens slightly." Are you interested in the classes?"

Considering that the one and only masterpiece I've created is a paint-by-number picture of a horse, I should probably consider taking an art class, but my schedule is full right now trying to save my reputation. "I'm very interested in the classes."

"Come with me." She gestures towards a desk sitting in the corner of the impressive gallery space. "We offer group lessons and the private ones, of course."

Of course she does. "I think I should start with the group lesson."

"Mrs. Mitchell always suggests private lessons if your budget allows," she whispers the words even though we are the only two people in the room. "If you're hoping to sell your work one day, it's really the best investment you can make in yourself."

Wrong. The best investment I can make in myself is finding out where the woman is so I can confront her and get this over with.

"Maybe I should speak to her about it first?" I toss it out as a question. "Is she going to be here soon?"

She looks around the room, her eyes surveying the space as if she expects to find someone lurking in a corner listening to the two of us. "She was supposed to be here an hour ago but she's meeting someone."

Considering the way her eyebrows are dancing around, I'm going to guess that Mrs. Mitchell isn't having a meeting with Mr. Mitchell.

"Gotcha." I wink at her. "She's beautiful. I bet a lot of the students who enroll in her classes are men."

She chuckles as she reaches for my arm. "They are but she's very choosy about who she gives private lessons to."

This woman is a master of hidden innuendo. "Is that where she is now? She's giving a private lesson to someone?"

She leans so close to me that I fear her lips are going to brush across mine when she speaks. "The man she's meeting right now is gorgeous. He's tall. He's got a sexy beard and his eyes are the most intense shade of blue you've ever seen."

Chapter 12

"I need to see Rowan Bell." I strum my fingers over the steel of the reception desk. "It's urgent."

"Ms. Bell is in an interview with someone right now," she literally spits the words out all over her computer monitor. "It's probably for the position you had before you quit."

You probably haven't gotten laid in forever. That's why you're such a bitch.

I want to say that but I need to get up to the thirty-seventh floor without Clive being alerted so I take a more subtle approach. "Can you call Dan in developments? I have a surprise for him."

"Dan?" she parrots back his name. "You want me to call Dan?"

It's seriously not that complicated. "Yes, I'd like for you to call Dan and ask him to come down to see me."

"Can't you just go up and see him yourself?"

It can't possibly be that easy to get past the hyped up security that Corteck is famous for. The biggest threat to their security isn't a random attack by a hacker, it's this woman right here. "I can go find him myself?"

"You used to work here." She gestures towards the elevators. "You know the way."

I nod. I do know the way. I know the route I need to take to finally confront the woman who is trying to ruin my life.

***

I only had to wait in the alcove by the elevator for ten minutes for Bruce to wander away from his desk. I know, based on what I saw when I went over the security systems with Jordan, that Bruce is supposed to lock the double glass doors that lead into where Clive's office is, if he ever has to leave his desk. Right now, there's no Bruce and no lock. Corteck apparently is on the cutting edge of incompetency and Mr. Parker is too preoccupied to realize that.

I stand just outside the closed doors of Clive's office. Judging by what I've seen since I arrived here, there's a very good chance that

I'll be able to walk right in. I'm beginning to doubt if the locks on the doors even work.

I push my ear to the door. I can only make out muffled voices. I know she's in there. All I need to do is swing open the door and ask them both what the hell is going on. I step back to run my hand through my hair. I'm wearing a simple green and blue striped dress. My intention was to swing by the gallery and then go in to work at Hughes just a few minutes late. Now, my entire day has been sucked into the vortex of chasing Clive's former lover around Manhattan.

I stare at the polished steel door handle. This is it. I reach for it, push it down and walk through.

They both turn to look at me at the very same moment. I can't take my eyes off of her though. She's tall, blonde and incredibly beautiful.

"Lilly?" Clive's hands leap from the pockets of his pants. "What are you doing here?"

I need to speak. In all of the imagined scenarios that raced through my mind, there wasn't one where I stood in place, frozen with anxiety. I planned this moment out with expert precision. I came here to confront her because after speaking with Parker, there's absolutely no doubt in my mind that this woman is behind what happened at the Hughes event.

I knew it without a shred of doubt when Parker asked me to send him another picture because he never had a chance to save a copy of the Polaroid I sent him.

It wasn't Clive. I may have doubted him at first, but after Parker told me this woman's name and I searched for her online, her connection to both Clive and Alec is clear. She's out for revenge and I'm just a tool to her.

"Lilly," Clive repeats my name as he pulls me into his chest. "Are you okay? Do you need something?"

I nod as I pull back from his embrace. "I need to talk to Allison."

Chapter 13

"You don't have any proof." She waves her perfectly manicured hand in my face. "You are just upset that the entire world saw your little tits."

They're not that little. I mean they're not big but they're at least a handful.

"Wow. Aren't you the definition of class?" I toss back because respecting your elders ceases to exist when they share your naked picture at a tech conference.

"What possible reason would I have to show that picture to anyone?"

It's a good question and right now, Allison Mitchell, sculptor and charity benefactor, thinks that she has the upper hand. When I did a search for her name online last night, every result was a beautiful image of her in an expensive dress or a glowing character reference from a business tycoon or celebrity. There's no doubt that the woman does amazing things for the charities of Manhattan. If you consider all the pictures of her hanging off the arms of the rich, single and attractive men of this city, you'd think that she has a life most women can only dream of. The problem is that she has a husband and two children.

"You were involved with Alec, weren't you?"

"What?" Clive finally re-enters our conversation. He'd taken a seat behind his desk after I told Allison that I knew she was the one who had sabotaged my presentation.

"She slept with Alec," I stop to correct myself. "She actually was in love with Alec."

"Alec Hughes?" she spits his name out with as much bitter disdain as she can conjure up. "You think I'd sleep with him?"

"I know you did."

"He's not even attractive," she throws the words back so fast my head almost spins.

"That's a weak argument." I lean back on my heel. "Alec is gorgeous."

I hear Clive clear his throat but his insecurities need to take a back seat. I'm going to push Allison into admitting what she did.

"I didn't sleep with Alec." She stomps her foot on the carpeted floor like a petulant child who can't have the last piece of candy. "Alec and I worked on a project together."

"Call it whatever the hell you want, lady." I roll my eyes. "Alec told me. He told me he dumped you when you went back to your husband for the second time."

"You were separated before?" Again, Clive picks the most inopportune time to chime in. Apparently, he and Allison didn't have any time to talk when they were banging each other.

"You were her third separation fling." I hold up three fingers to drill the point in. "She's actually still technically separated."

"You know that I love you, Clive." She turns towards him as she purrs the words. "Any other man meant nothing to me."

I look at Clive. His gaze is riveted to me. "How did you find out all of this?"

I ignore the question because it's not a discussion I want to have in front of his former lover. I turn back towards her even though her eyes are glued to him. "Why did you put that picture of me in the slideshow?"

"I told you that I had nothing to do with that."

"I showed Cheryl a picture of you," I almost scream the words into her face. "She said it was you."

"She's lying," she says too calmly. "The old cow is lying."

"You're lying," I snap back. When Lance had called me last night to ask me how I was doing, I'd asked for Cheryl's full name. He told it to me without any hesitation at all. It was unusual enough to be distinguishable from most of Manhattan. After finding her address online, I'd taken the subway to her apartment. I knocked on her door and showed her a picture of Allison on my phone and she'd confessed the entire thing. I'd like to believe it was because I looked so threatening in my oversized sweater and jeans. That wasn't what pushed her over the crevice and into a confession. It was the fact that Alec had explained my past to her and the motherly parts of her couldn't stand the guilt. She not only admitted to everything, she quit her job too.

"You have no proof," she pulls each of the words over her teeth. "It's my word against her word."

"You gave that woman a few thousand dollars and the promise of a week-long vacation at your estate in Hawaii in exchange for her to slip my picture into the slideshow."

She recoils physically with the words. "I can't believe she told you all of that."

"I can't believe you'd use me to hurt the men you've been fucking."

Her hand flies in the air but I'm quick to grab her wrist. Clive is on his feet and rounding his desk before either of us has time to react. Allison pulls her arm free of my grip and lunges into his arms.

"Clive," she whispers into his chest. "I was so upset that you dumped me for that. I wasn't thinking straight at all."

"What the fuck were you trying to accomplish?" He's holding tight to her shoulders, shaking her gently with each word. "Do you know what you've done?"

"You can forgive me for this." She pats the side of his cheek. "We were having so much fun before she came along."

"Why did you take a picture of the Polaroid in the first place?" I step towards them both. "Why would you do that?"

She doesn't respond. She only ups the volume on her exaggerated sobs as she clings to him.

"Allison." His voice is calm. It's so calm. "Tell me what happened."

"You'll forgive me if I do?"

His head moves up and down briefly. The motion is so slight and minute that it's almost indistinguishable.

"You came back with Parker after going to see her that night." Her head turns towards me briefly before she settles her gaze back on him. "I heard you telling him to leave her alone. You said he wasn't good enough for Lilly."

I listen intently. This is a birds-eye-view of what happened that night.

"When he left, you told me that you were going to book me a flight back to Manhattan." The words escape her in a rush. "I didn't want to go back, remember?"

"I remember that, yes." His eyes are focused completely on her face.

"I went to powder my nose and when I came back you were staring at it," she says gruffly. "You were just staring at her body in that picture."

Chapter 14

"So you took the picture of Lilly's photograph when I went to get your things from the bedroom?"

They're sitting together on the couch now. Not more than a few inches separate the two of them. I'm not even sure, at this point whether either of them remembers that I'm in the room.

"I just wanted to have a copy," she says softly, under her breath.

"Why did you give it to Cheryl?" He leans forward until his eyes catch hers. "Tell me why you did that, Allie."

I wince when I hear him call her that. It speaks of familiarity and fondness. He's never called me anything but Lilly and the knowledge of that bites into me.

"Before we went to Boston and you ended things, we agreed to talk a few weeks later about the charity fundraiser for the emergency shelter." She touches his knee and he doesn't pull back.

"That was the same night you saw me in my office with Lilly?"

"I called out to you when you were walking into your office, but you didn't hear me." Tears fall down her cheeks. "You rushed to the window to where she was."

My stomach knots so tightly that the sheer force of it almost causes me to double over in pain. She was there, in the background, watching us as Clive brought me to an orgasm with his fingers. She'd watched the entire thing. I thought that she walked up to the doorway after our intimate encounter was over.

"I saw what happened." Her voice is almost a shrill wail now. "I saw you touching her and I heard when she…"

I'm grateful that she doesn't say the words aloud. She doesn't need to.

"Did you give Cheryl the picture to get back at me for that?" He pulls back slightly, his arm flying over the back of the couch to gain distance from her.

"I wanted her to go back to Boston." Her fingers dart into the air in my direction. "I wanted you to come back to me."

"Why did you do it at Alec's event?" I jump in from where I'm standing across the room.

Clive's gaze locks on mine. I can't read anything he's feeling.

"I want to know why you didn't just release it to the press and leave it at that." My voice takes on a hard edge. "Why do it right before I announced my app?"

She looks at the side of Clive's face before her eyes fall to her lap. She takes a moment to smooth her hands over the skirt of the red dress she's wearing. "I knew that it would humiliate you to see the picture up on that big screen."

She's right. It would have been impossible for me not to feel as though I'd never recover from that moment. "Did you tell Cheryl when it should pop up? I mean, did you know it would come up right before I announced my own app?"

She nods briskly, her hand leaping to Clive's thigh. "When Cheryl showed me the other slides on that flash drive you gave her, I knew you were launching that organ donation app to impress Clive because of what happened to his sister. God rest her soul."

Clive pushes himself to his feet. "You don't know anything, Allison. You seriously don't know what the fuck you're talking about."

"I do know." She holds out her hand waiting for him to grab it, but he just stares at it.

"You could have ruined her entire career." Clive's hands are fisting at his sides. "Do you see the damage you've done?"

She bolts to her feet in one swift and elegant movement. "She's fine. She's young. She can get a job back in Boston."

I take a heavy step towards them both. "I have a job here. I'm still working for Alec."

"Alec was never very smart," she hisses the words at me. "He'll give anything a chance as long as it has a pussy."

Chapter 15

Clive's face twists at the vulgarity of her words. "That's a disgusting thing to say."

"It's true," she tosses back flippantly. "Alec gave her that job because he wants to fuck her. It's the same reason you gave her a job."

He charges towards her, grabbing her shoulders with both of his hands. "Shut up, Allison. You need to shut up."

"You're not stupid enough to believe that Alec doesn't want a taste of that, are you?"

"Don't talk about her like that." He shakes her gently. "You don't know what you're talking about."

"I was there." She pokes her index finger into the white dress shirt that is covering his rock hard chest. "I was at the media event. Alec was practically drooling over her picture. If he hasn't fucked her yet, he's going to."

I'm tempted to march over and pull her hair back so hard her neck snaps. I don't move though. I can't. She's lost all control and every vile thing that is flying out of her dark red lips is pushing her deeper into the hole she's digging for herself.

"Alec is getting married," Clive points out. "He didn't hire Lilly so he could fuck her."

"You're not as smart as you think you are." She pats his bearded chin. "You can't put a young thing like that in front of a man like Alec and expect him to stay faithful."

"Alec doesn't see me like that," I finally interject. "You're wrong about him."

"Alec jumped into bed with a girl your age when he was fucking me." She states that random fact back to me with pride. "I caught him feasting on her pussy on his desk in his office. I saw it with my own two eyes."

Those are details I didn't need to know. I've sat right in front of that desk. I hope I didn't touch it.

"You've put my entire career at risk." I feel a desperate need to change the subject. "You need to be held accountable for that."

Her head rolls back in laughter. "Do you honestly think anyone in their right mind would believe that I would do anything to hurt you?"

I stare at her, marveling in how oblivious she is to what she's done to my life. "I believe they'd have to. I have proof that you did it."

"You have the word of a woman who has accomplished next to nothing in her life," she pauses before she continues. "My word trumps Cheryl's word any day of the week."

I can't argue that point because it's true. Allison is on the board of virtually every major charity event in the city. She volunteers her time to help people all over the state and half of the proceeds of the sale of her art, goes directly into a fund that provides scholarships for at risk teens. The woman is a saint in the eyes of the press.

"If Lilly's picture shows up anywhere online, I'll tell Luther." Clive's voice is deep and measured. "I will tell him who you've been fucking and I'll give him enough ammunition that your shared custody agreement will change dramatically."

"You're threatening me with my children?"

"You rarely see them as it is, Allison." He darts his finger into the air so it hovers near her face. "That's by your choice. If you don't clean up this mess you've made, I'll have no choice but to go to your husband and tell him everything."

In my quest to find every detail I could about Allison Mitchell, I'd been bombarded with information about her husband. He is older, very accomplished and very devoted to her. His face beamed as he stared at her in every photograph of the two of them I ran across. Luther Mitchell is clearly a man in love with a woman he can't tame.

"I'll see to it that Lilly's picture disappears." She runs her long fingers through her hair. "If anyone prints it, I'll handle it."

Chapter 16

"There's a question sitting right there." He leans forward to brush his full, soft lips over mine. "Ask me, Lilly."

I instantly taste the bourbon. He'd downed a half glass of it after he'd sent Allison on her way. I'd watched in silence as she tried to embrace him but he'd held her off with his hands on her shoulders, telling her that Bruce would handle any meetings related to charities in the future. He essentially cut her off and all she could do was stand there and accept it.

"Did you sleep with her after I left your office that night?"

His left brow cocks up. "You mean that night I touched you? The night you came on my hand?"

I nod. I remember the casual way they sat together on the couch as I was leaving. The fact that she dropped her hand onto his thigh seemed flirtatious at the time. Now, with the added knowledge of their past, it seems like it was a prelude to something more.

"I haven't fucked another woman since I saw you in Boston at the bistro."

"She still wanted you when she came to your office that night." I blow out a puff of air in an exaggerated effort to calm down. "I saw how she touched you."

"She wanted more." He nods in agreement as he scoops my hand into his. "I wanted nothing to do with her."

I believe him. I don't doubt anything he's telling me. "I was just wondering."

"Sit with me for a minute." He gestures towards the couch. "I want to tell you something."

I follow without any resistance at all. I finally feel as though I can breathe for the first time in days. My thoughts are no longer the muddled mess they've been. I know, without any question, that the words he's said to me in the past have been grounded in truth.

I sit down on the couch, crossing my legs carefully. "What do you want to tell me?"

"I'm very impressed by what you did, Lilly." He rests his hand on my knee. "I don't know how to explain it but I'll try."

I stare at his face as my hand wanders to my chest. I trace my fingers over the skin of my neck. I stare at his mouth waiting for him to speak and wanting desperately for him to kiss me again.

He pulls my hand back into his, resting it on his thigh. "You used to wear a necklace, didn't you?"

I close my eyes briefly. "How do you know that?"

"You reach for it all the time." His tone is warm. "I also saw a picture in your office at Hughes this morning. It's a picture of you and your mother."

After Alec had given me my own office, I'd taken a few things there to make it more personal. It was a corporate corner that essentially belonged to me and I wanted to be reminded of that every day when I arrived at work. The picture of my mother and I had been taken on my fourteenth birthday. She was beaming as she stood next to me and I proudly wore the chain and pendant she had custom made just for me. In the chaos of the night my family was taken from me, the necklace had been pulled from my neck when the paramedics were trying to control the bleeding. I searched frantically for it when I was released from the hospital, but it was nowhere to be found.

"You were at my office today?" I ask, turning my head to look at him.

"I wanted to see you," he confesses tenderly. "I was desperate to see you. After you walked out of my place on Saturday, I was aching to be near you."

He'd called me a few times yesterday but I'd ignored them all. Part of it was my immersion in trying to identify who broadcast my picture but the bigger, and more honest part of it, was something entirely different. I was pissed at him. He wouldn't tell me her name when I demanded it.

"Why wouldn't you tell me it was Allison?" I twist my body around so I'm facing him directly. "You were protecting her."

It's more accusatory than I want it to be. The words may sound bitter but the emotion behind them is grounded in something else. I'm not jealous of Allison. She fucked Clive and in the big picture of his world, she's just one woman who crawled into his bed and his life for a time. I'm hurt that when my life was spinning out of my control, Clive didn't trust me with the name of the person he suspected set me into that turmoil. He effectively chose her over me and any argument he tosses my way can't justify what he did.

"I was protecting her children," he corrects me and silences my questions all in one short sentence. "Allison is a horrible mother. Her children deserve better."

"I can see your point, Clive." I push my shoulders back. "But did you really think I was going to rush over to her place and out her in front of her kids?"

"No." He dips his chin towards me. "I know you better than that. You'd never compromise a child for any reason."

He's right. It's not something I'd do to Allison's children or anyone's. "Why then? All you had to do was tell me her name. I don't think you know how much that would have helped me."

"I do know. I also know that you're concerned about how the fiasco with your picture is going to impact Alec's business."

"I am," I agree. "I'm very worried about that."

"I knew that if I told you about Allison that there was a very good chance you'd talk to Alec about it." He reaches to run his fingers over my bare knee. "Alec has no self-control. I had some concern that someone from his organization would decide the best approach would be to call Allison out in public."

"In public?"

"Alec's shameless. He's reckless." He gestures with his chin towards his smartphone on the table near us. "He sent out a mass email once when he caught one of his employees stealing from petty cash. He fired the guy and made his life a living hell."

I can't say that I'm that surprised by any of it. Alec is bold and brash and judging by the success of his business, his approach hasn't failed him yet.

"You're very strong, Lilly." He chuckles slightly. "It's the truth but it's an understatement."

I'm touched by the compliment but I don't want it to derail the conversation. "You should have told me about her. We could have talked about whether I needed to tell Alec."

"Part of why I'm crazy about you is your vulnerability." He touches his chest. "You feel everything so deeply. You've lived through so much and it hasn't made you jaded at all. You're not like me in that sense."

I can't argue with that. Clive can shift from loving and caring with me to brutal businessman with others on the turn of a dime. He's ruthless and calculating. Those aren't qualities I aspire to. I never want to be like him in those ways. "I don't need to be like you in that way."

"You're right about that." He winks at me. "If I would have given you Allison's name, you would have confronted her on your own without me or Alec there."

"You're right," I agree with a brisk nod of my head. "I would have called her out on her bullshit."

"I know that." His mouth slides into a sly grin. "I absolutely know that but the woman is pure evil. She would have said things to you. She would have lashed out and hurt you. I didn't want that. I couldn't stomach the thought of that."

I should be at least mildly offended by the fact that he didn't view me as strong enough to go face-to-face with Allison. That's not what I feel at all. I feel treasured and adored. He was trying to protect me. "I can stand up for myself, Clive."

"You don't have to convince me of that." He runs his hand over his chin. "Remind me never to mess with you in the future."

"Please don't take my choices away like that again." I cross my arms over my chest. "I had a right to deal with this on my own. It's my picture and I'm the one who set everything in motion when I sent it to Parker."

He slides his body closer to mine. "I'm sorry. I didn't see it that way at all. I thought I was protecting you. I didn't want you hurt any more than you had been."

"Tell me that you get that I can handle stuff on my own." The words themselves may sound bratty and impetuous, but they are grounded in something more than that. "I need to take care of myself. It's just how I am."

He scratches his finger alongside his nose. "I've never doubted that for a minute, Lilly. I want you to know that and understand it. I didn't try and control the situation because of my own needs. I just didn't want you hurt."

Arguing against his need to care for me seems foolish. It's what I've craved since I understood that not all relationships between a man and a woman were built on a foundation of anger, violence and animosity. "I'm going to get hurt sometimes."

"Not if I have my way." He pulls me closer. "I'll destroy anyone who tries to hurt you."

I lean into his chest, knowing that every word he speaks is the absolute truth.

Chapter 17

"We can't do that in your office." I push against his chest in vain. "I don't think we should do that here."

"I locked the door, Lilly." He pushes my dress from my shoulders. "No one will interrupt us."

"We can wait and do it tonight." I straighten my arms so the dress can fall to the floor beside where he's already tossed my panties.

"We're going to do this again tonight." His lips chart a most path over my shoulder from behind. "Tonight you're going to wrap that beautiful mouth of yours around my cock until I blow my load all over your face."

My sex clenches at the promise of a taste of him again. "I can do it now."

"No." His hand snakes around me, landing on the front clasp of the black lace bra I'm wearing. "Now, I'm going to lick your pretty wet cunt."

"Oh, God," I say as I look down to see him snapping the clasp open.

"Your breasts are so beautiful." He brings both hands to them, kneading the tender flesh before he pulls softly on the nipples. "They're so sensitive."

They are. Just the touch of his fingers on the swollen buds is making me aroused. I know that the moment I feel his tongue on my core, that my body will rock into an intense orgasm. "I want you to fuck me."

"You can feel my cock, can't you?" His voice is deep and rich. "You can feel how hard it is."

I gasp when I hear the unmistakable sound of his zipper being pulled down. I moan loudly when he pushes me forward so he can glide the lush swollen head over my pussy. "Please, just do it."

"Sit down, Lilly." His hand dips to my wetness and he flicks my clit with a quick touch of his index finger. "I'm going to lick this."

I practically fall out of my heels as I lunge towards the couch. I spin around, opening my legs as an invitation as he lowers himself to his knees. His large, erect cock bobs up and down through his open pants. I can see the vein that snakes up the side. I want to run my tongue over it. I want to pull it into my mouth and taste his release.

"This is mine." He lazily runs his tongue over my folds and I flinch. "This is all just for me."

"Yes," I whisper as I weave my fingers into his hair. "It's all yours."

"Tell me how badly you want it." He licks the entire length of my sex, stopping to press his tongue into me. "Tell me now."

"I want it so much." The words escape in a moan. I pull harder on his hair, desperately trying to guide his mouth to me. "Just do it."

"You taste so good." He lowers his mouth again, using his tongue to circle the swollen center of my pleasure. I arch my back and push my hips off the couch to feel more.

"You're so greedy." He licks his index finger before sliding it into my channel. "I can feel how badly you want to come."

My hips rock against his hand. "I need to come."

His eyes catch mine for a brief second before he pulls my clit between his lips. He sucks on it hard. I buck under him, everything disappearing except my desperate need to find my release. I call out his name, not caring if anyone can hear. I can't contain any of this.

He sucks harder, his finger sliding in and out with expert precision. I grind myself into his face, pulling on his hair, pushing against him.

"Lilly, Christ, I love this."

I come when I hear the words. I cry out his name over and over as I fall into the orgasm. I cling to his hair, my hand racing down his cheek to cup his moist chin. I want him to stop. I need him inside of me.

"Please, fuck me, please." The words drip with all the wanton pleasure I feel.

He's on his feet in an instant, rounding his desk to open a drawer. I watch his every move, memorized by the fluidity of his body. His eyes never leave mine as he sheds the rest of his clothes and sheathes his thick cock.

He pulls my legs into the air, positioning himself above me. "You're so fucking tight. You take me so deep."

I reach up, wanting to grab hold of him in any way I can.

He senses my need and leans forward." I need you, Lilly. You don't know how badly I need you."

I nod. My voice is lost. I want to give in to it all. I want to express what I feel too. "Please, Clive. Please."

He pushes his lips into mine, his tongue darting into my mouth as his cock slides into me slowly, painfully and fully.

I bury my scream into his breath. I cling tightly to him as he rocks his hips into me. "I love fucking you. I love it."

I moan loudly when he ups the tempo. His cock pounds harder into me with each thrust. "It's so good," I cry out.

"Lilly." My name falls from his lips in a heated whisper. "Christ, Lilly."

I close my eyes as he pushes his hand under my ass to curve my body into his. The friction only spurs me on more. I grind my hips up and into his with each heated plunge.

"I'll never let you go," he whispers the words into my cheek. "I can't let you go."

I move my head to catch his lips with mine. "Never, "I whisper back.

He pulls back, slamming his cock into me over and over again. My back arches when I feel my body nearing its edge. I cling to his hips, crying out because it feels so good.

I writhe beneath him as the orgasm washes over me. He pumps through it, groaning as he feels my sex clench around him.

"Yes," he calls gently into the air between us. He grinds his hips into me fiercely as slides into his own release.

Chapter 18

"Your balls are twice the size of Lance's balls."

It's a compliment. I know it doesn't exactly come across that way but it's Alec Hughes and it's the way he doles out praise. "Thanks, Alec."

"You kicked Allison's skinny ass." He nods towards my computer. "The shopping app is doing great. You've had a pretty good week considering."

I smile at the veiled reference to what happened almost a week ago now. I've been back at work for a few days, and focused on developing yet another new app for the company. This one is centered on pet care and with all the advantages it has over what's already on the market, I know it's going to be a huge hit for Hughes.

"I'm sorry I haven't been in the office the last few days." He inches closer to my desk. "I took a few Libby days."

"Libby days?" I grin broadly.

"I can't get enough of that woman." He rolls his eyes. "I could sit and watch her eat toast and it would be the most interesting part of my day."

That's another pure Alec comment. "Libby is really lucky."

"She knows it." He cocks a brow. "I'd say Clive is lucky too but the guy doesn't deserve you."

The wide grin on his face is all I need to see to know that he's teasing me. He called Clive last night when I was at his condo having dinner with him. The two had bantered back and forth about an upcoming conference in San Francisco that they're both attending. I'd sat back and listened, lifted by the smile on Clive's face as he called Alec an asshole.

"You and Clive are okay now?"

"We're getting there," I say truthfully. I've worked late most of this week to keep my mind in a positive place. Although I came back to a few jeers and stares from some of my male co-workers, over all everyone has been supportive and kind. "I'm meeting him for lunch today."

His head darts past me to where a small clock hangs on the wall. It's a remnant left from the last person who had this office, and likely the person before that, but I think it's charming, even though the white plastic that surrounds the face has turned a weathered yellow. "It's almost one. What time is this lunch date?"

"Why?" I volley back. "Are you going to tag along?"

"I will if it's at Axel. They just put some new sandwiches on their menu."

Three's a crowd but seeing as how Alec has been so supportive to me, I do the cordial thing. "It's at Axel. You can come with us if you want."

He scratches his head through the thick black, messy hair. "I better not. The owner is my best friend. I think he's in town. I owe him a beer and once I sit down with the guy we never stop talking."

"Your best friend is Hunter Reynolds?" I should actually sound more surprised than I do. I'm beginning to understand that New York is actually smaller than I thought. Everyone knows Hunter Reynolds.

"You've met him?"

"Briefly," I mutter. "I just saw him once when I was there with some friends."

"Have you met his wife?"

"Sadie? I haven't." I glance at my computer screen. "I guess I should go if I'm going to meet Clive on time."

"You'd like Sadie." He turns to walk out of my office. "I think you'd be really good friends."

***

"Clive told me about you, Lilly." She lets go of my hand. "I'm really impressed with the work you've been doing."

I look at Clive's smiling face before I glide my eyes back to Sadie. She's lovely. She's a little bit older than I am and the top of the scar on her chest is visible over the neckline of her sweater. She's radiant. "Clive has told me about you too. He says you're studying to be a doctor."

"I'm trying," she pauses. "I just had a baby so I'm trying to juggle a lot."

I know it can't be easy for Clive to see the woman who has his sister's heart within her body, living a very full and happy life. I drop my hand to his on his lap and squeeze it tightly.

"Did you have a boy or a girl?" I ask, not just because it's expected but also because I'm interested.

"A daughter." Her face brightens even more. "Her name is Olivia. She's so beautiful."

"It's such a pretty name."

"Cory picked it out." She smiles at Clive. "He's a great big brother."

"He's the best," he chimes in. "I have some books I meant to bring with me for Cory but I'll be in Boston next weekend and I can drop them off then."

Her face twists into a mix of panic and excitement. "Hunter and I wanted to talk to you about that."

I feel Clive's hand tense in mine. He's had to endure a lot to be able to maintain a relationship with his biological nephew. He adores the boy and judging by Sadie's foreboding words, there may be trouble brewing. "What's going on, Sadie?"

She rubs the growing perspiration from her forehead. "Hunter is in a meeting. I'd rather wait for him before we discuss this."

"If it's about Cory, I want to know now." He's working hard to quiet the anxiety in his tone. "Please, Sadie. Just tell me."

Her eyes drift over my face. "You know Dr. Foster, don't you, Lilly?"

"Dr. Foster? Is Cory sick?" Clive's hand drops mine. "Sadie, he's sick again, isn't he?"

Her hand leaps to her chest. "No. I'm sorry. No, he's perfect. He's great."

"Dr. Foster is my friend," I offer. "How do you know that?"

"I met Ben yesterday. We were talking about organ donation and he mentioned his friend, Lilly."

It's misplaced and intimate. I had no idea that Ben spoke about me to anyone. "I met Ben in a grief support group a long time ago."

"He told me that." She reaches over the table to touch my hand. "When he said your name was Lilly, I told him my friend, Clive, was dating a Lilly and we put it together and here you are now."

The circle of my life keeps getting bigger and bigger. I had no friends beyond my roommate and the manager of the bistro back in Boston. Now fate is gifting me with so many new faces, all of them connected in some way. "I can't believe you met Ben."

"Clive." She turns her attention towards him even though she doesn't let go of my hand. "Cory misses you so much."

"I miss him a lot too," he says in a hushed tone.

"Hunter has to come here so often." She shakes her head with a smile. "He's in New York more than Boston at this point."

Clive chuckles. "I was going to suggest you just move here."

She pulls in a breath. It's not helping to ward off the tears that are filling her brown eyes. "That's the thing. We are. We're moving to New York."

Clive is on his feet and without missing a beat, he pulls Sadie up and into his arms. "You're bringing Cory here? He's going to be here?"

"He's coming, Olivia too and the dog." She laughs as she leans into his chest.

"That's amazing. It's so fucking amazing." He kisses the top of her head. "Thank you, Sadie. Thank you."

"You need to thank Lilly's friend, Ben." She nods towards me, her arms still wrapped tightly around Clive. "He's the one who gave me a job working at the hospital."

Chapter 19

"Your app has been downloaded more than two thousand times." He hands me a bottle of water as I sit in one of the chairs in his living room. It's Saturday afternoon and we're both stealing the day away from work.

"The shopping app?"

"Your app." His lips brush softly over mine. "The organ donation app."

"What?" I reach for his cheek to stop him from pulling away. "What do you mean? How is that possible?"

"Alec and I decided to launch the app the day you were going to introduce it at the media event." He pulls my hand to his mouth. "We uploaded it to a few different platforms and it's gone viral."

"My app?" I feel the need to clarify the point again. "You're shitting me."

A brilliant smile pulls at the corners of his lips. "I'm not shitting you."

"It wasn't ready for market yet." I look into his face. "I hadn't finished with the testing, and I didn't choose a name, and..."

"I looked it over for you." He squeezes my hand. "I know it wasn't my place, but I wanted something good to come out of the media event and that app is brilliant, Lilly. I put it up to test it to see if it had any viability or needed improvement."

"I want to see." I motion towards my smartphone on the coffee table. "Can I see?"

He hands me his phone. "Check on mine. I created an account for you. You can change the log-in details to what you want, but it's open and there for you to look right now. I was going to wait to surprise you when we got to five thousand downloads, but I have no patience."

I scroll my finger across the screen and open the browser. I stare at the numbers. "Clive, it's close to three thousand units."

"You're on fire. It was two thousand last night." He dips his head down to look at the screen. "You're going to change so many lives."

"It says the app is called..." The emotion that hits me feels like a tidal wave. I push my shoulders forward trying to curb the rush of tears. "Perla. You named it Perla."

"Yes. I named it after the most beautiful woman in the world." He's in front of me now, his hands holding tightly to my legs. "I named the app after you."

My hand leaps to my neck, in search of the beautiful necklace my mother had given me. The name Perla crafted from silver had hung on a delicate chain.

"No one knows that my name is Perla," I whisper the words into his cheek. "No one but my mother called me that."

"It's such a beautiful name." He reaches to take his phone from my hand. "I realized it was your birth name when I read about the shooting. I've never heard it before."

"She chose all of our names. My sister was named Briella. My brothers were named River and Reave."

"They're all so unique and special." He rests his forehead against mine. "Did you change your name to Lilly after the shooting?"

"Legally, yes. I was trying to escape what happened and it seemed like the best way at the time." I nod slowly. "When I was young. I don't remember when but maybe when I was seven or eight, the kids at school would tease me about my name."

"Kids can be cruel." He kisses the tip of my nose. "Imagine being a boy named Clive."

I pull my hand up to my mouth to stifle a laugh. "I came home from school one day and told my mother that I hated my name."

It's a memory that I still struggle with. The pain of disappointment had been clear within her eyes. She'd held back tears.

"What did she say?" he asks softly.

"She said that she could pick a new name for me if I wanted," I say, sniffling. "I told her that's exactly what I wanted."

"She chose Lilly." His brows rise. "It's equally as beautiful as Perla."

"She loved the flower so much." I touch my chest. "She'd get tears in her eyes when we'd bring her a bouquet on her birthday."

"She sounds like she was an amazing woman, Lilly." His voice cracks. "I'm sorry I never got to meet her."

"I am too." I don't try to stop the tears. "I am too."

Chapter 20

"That was the longest weekend of my entire life." Clive motions for the driver to stop. "Remind me never to go to a conference with Alec again."

I nod, knowing that they have plans to have a beer at the end of the week. Lance told me that he saw it on Alec's calendar. "Why didn't we go back to your place?"

"You can't wait to crawl all over me, can you?" He licks his lips. "We need to make this one stop and then we'll go."

I gaze out the window. The driver has pulled up next to the curb on a street I've never been on. "Is this a business thing? Can't it wait until tomorrow?"

"It's a Lilly thing and it can't wait." He motions for me to exit the car once the driver opens the door.

"A Lilly thing?"

"We'll be a few minutes." Clive looks at the driver. "Wait here."

"Are we going shopping?" I stomp my heeled foot against the sidewalk. It's near eight now and I have an early morning conference call with Alec and a team of developers in Italy. I've worked hard on preparing my presentation and a good night's sleep is an absolute must. I know I'm not likely to get that once Clive gets me into his bed, but after we make love, I have to try and rest for at least a few hours.

"We're picking something up." He motions towards the glass doors of a small shop. "It's this way."

I follow his lead as he holds the door open for me. I walk into a beautiful, bright space. My eyes soak in the rows of jewelry display cases and the vibrant watercolor paintings that decorate the space. It's elegant and understated.

"Clive." A petite blonde woman rushes over. "You're finally here."

"Ivy." He embraces her quickly. "How are you?"

"I'm good." She rests her hands on his cheeks. "I like the beard. You look great."

"Hands off my cousin, Ivy." A tall man, carrying a small boy walks into my line of sight. "Hey, Clive."

"Jax." He extends his hand with a nod of his head. "How's Jackson?"

"Busy," Ivy interjects. "He keeps us so busy."

Clive nods as he reaches for my hand. "This is my Lilly."

"Lilly," Ivy embraces me fully, pulling my body into hers. "I'm so glad to meet you. When Clive told me about you, I knew you'd be beautiful."

"I'm sorry," Clive's voice is low. "This is my cousin Jax and his wife Ivy. That's Jackson, right there."

I pull back from the embrace to smile at them all. "I'm really happy to meet you."

"Can I give it to her now?" Ivy taps Clive on his chest. "I'm going to explode if I can't give it to her now."

"Go get it." He clasps her hands in his. "Now is perfect."

She scurries away in her heels, the rhythmic clicking of them on the floor the only sound in the quiet space.

"Ivy designs jewelry," Jax offers. "This is her shop and studio."

"She's Ivy Marlow, isn't she?" My eyes dart up to Clive's face. "I've seen her pieces in magazines."

"Ivy Marlow- Walker," Jax corrects me. "Ivy forgets the Walker part but I remind her."

"Clive wanted me to make this for you, Lilly." Ivy is back with a long, rectangular box in her hand. "I was honored that he asked me to do it."

I'm going to cry. I'm going to open the box and whatever is in there is going to push me off the edge of this emotional cliff I'm standing on. I've just met more of Clive's family and they've opened their arms to me. Now, I have to open a box that will hold something beautiful made by the hands of someone he cares about.

"Are you okay, Lilly?" Clive's arm is around my shoulder. "I wanted to get you something special."

"It's not my birthday," I say to spare me another moment to catch my breath. "It's not."

"I don't need an excuse to give you things." His lips brush over my forehead. "You deserve beautiful things every day."

My hands are shaking as I pull open the lid of the box. I close my eyes, wanting to curb the rush of emotions that will overwhelm me if I see what I'm expecting within the beautiful white box.

"Clive told us about your family." Ivy's voice breaks through the silence. "We talked about what we could make that would honor them."

I open my eyes. There's a thin silver chain that runs the length of the box. At the end is a pendant. It's edges are round, the surface a brushed silver. The engraved letters are simple and elegant each woven seamlessly into the next. From an uneducated eye it would appear to be a beautiful sweep of curves but to me its meaning is deeper and more thoughtful.

"Each letter is for a member of your family. You can see one R there, and another there," she begins before she points her nail at the sweep of engraving. "I put a B there for your sister and that's the P for you. Your mom was your mom, so I put an M for her."

I nod through my tears. "It's so beautiful. I've never seen anything this beautiful before."

"Thank you for asking me to do this for you." Ivy reaches onto her tiptoes to kiss Clive's cheek. "I'll never forget being a part of something so special."

***

"Mr. Parker, please." I pull against the silk ties that Clive slipped over my wrists when we first got into bed. We'd kissed in the car all the way back from the jewelry store. I was overcome with emotion and now I'm overcome with desire.

"I told you I was going to do this, Lilly." He's hovering over me, his hands pressing into the mattress on either side of my head. "Is this your first time?"

I look up to where he's secured the ties to the headboard. "No, I was tied up by…"

He kisses me deeply to silence the words. "Don't tell me about him," he growls into my mouth.

"You asked," I counter as I bite his bottom lip. "I'm the one who first suggested this at the bistro."

"My cock was rock hard that night." He drags his tongue over my lips. "When you said you liked to be tied up, I almost threw you over my shoulder and took you home with me."

"You should have," I whisper against his mouth. "We wouldn't have wasted so much time."

He moans loudly as I adjust my body beneath him. "You're so fucking wet."

"You do that to me." I pull on my hands again. "You make me feel things I haven't felt before."

He leans back to stroke his cock. "Tell me what I make you feel."

I look down and catch a glimpse of his large hand, dragging over the length of the thick root. "I want to suck it."

"You're so greedy, Lilly." He leans back even more to give me a better view. "You love sucking it, don't you?"

"I want to taste you."

"Tell me what I make you feel." He's stroking faster now.

"Please don't come like that. I want you to come on my face."

"Christ." He slows the pace slightly. "If you talk like that I'm going to shoot my load all over your breasts."

My legs twitch beneath him. "I want to come too."

"You will." He shifts his entire body until he's next to me. "Can I taste it now?"

"Do you want me, Lilly?" His voice is soft and warm now.

I look directly at his face. "What?"

"Do you want me?" he repeats, louder this time.

I don't know how to answer that other than with the absolute truth. "I want you so much."

He moves closer, the lush tip of his cock trails over my lips. "Open your mouth."

I lick my lips before I part them. I can't control the loud moan as he slides the tip of his cock into my mouth. I push my cheek into the soft sheet, wanting to take as much of him into me as I possibly can.

"It's so good." He cradles the back of my head. "You suck it so good."

I take the encouragement and offer even more. I bob my head slowly, taking in more with each movement. I groan when I feel him swell under my tongue.

"I love this. I fucking love how good you make me feel."

I suck loudly, the sounds of my mouth sliding over his cock filling the empty space of the room. I don't care about anything but his pleasure. I want him to give it to me. I want to taste every last drop of it.

"I'm so close." He growls into the air. "I can't stand how good it is."

I pull on the bindings, wishing I could free my hand to cup his heavy balls. I moan loudly in a combination of frustration and pure need.

He moves faster and harder, fucking my mouth with quick and easy strokes.

I feel his cock swell and his body tense. It's close. He's going to come. I let out a low hum that I know will add to the sensation.

He pulls back, his hands lost in my hair as he levels the tip of his cock at my lips. "I'm coming. Fuck, it's there."

I feel the first spurt as it hits my cheek. I adjust my head even though the bite of pleasure that comes from his hands in my hair is intense. I pull him into my mouth and take in everything he offers me.

Chapter 21

"I loved every minute of that." He's wrapped me into his arms now. After he came, he pulled me out of the ties and dropped to his knees to kiss me. "I want you just like this."

I should be disappointed that I didn't orgasm but I'm not. "I love being like this with you."

"I'll help you come in a little while." His voice is a whisper against my neck. "I'll lick your beautiful body. I'll do that all night."

I want to tell him that it's not what I need right now. My emotions are still right at the surface after he gave me the necklace. It was a beautiful gesture and one that speaks of his feelings for me. I want to tell him how I feel too but I'd need to do that with words and I'm not sure if I'm ready for that yet.

"I love the necklace so much." My hand moves to my neck and I cradle the pendant in my palm. "I can't believe how beautiful it is."

He moves his body so he can lean on one elbow and look down at me. "I thought about asking Ivy to recreate the necklace your mother gave you but…"

"I'm grateful that you didn't," I interrupt him. "That was something special she had made for me. This is something special you had made for me."

"I spoke to Ivy about it." He covers my hand that is cradling the pendant with his own. "I couldn't have come up with that design on my own."

"It's very thoughtful." I nuzzle my head under his neck. "It's just so beautiful. I love it."

"It's only the start." He pulls me closer to him. "I'm going to give you beautiful things as often as I can."

"You're going to spoil me." I move slightly so I can look into his eyes. "You don't have to spoil me."

"I'm not spoiling you, Lilly." His lips graze over mine. "I'm treasuring you. You are a gift to me. You're the greatest gift I've ever received."

"I didn't know my life could be like this," I say softly. "I never thought I could be happy."

"When you came into my life I didn't think that happiness could exist for me," he pauses to touch my chin. "I never realized that I could care this much for a woman. It just didn't seem like something I was capable of."

I could see that within him back then. He had a wall that mirrored my own around his heart. He was protecting it and hiding so closely behind it that no one could get in. "I didn't know that I could care about anyone this much either."

"You're it for me, Lilly Randall."

"I'm it for you?" I try to suppress the flood of tears that I know are about to spill out.

"I'm falling in love with you." He brushes his lips over mine. "No, that's not right."

My hand leaps to his cheek. "You can't take it back like that. You can't say it and then take it back."

He scoops my hand into his, sliding it over his beard to rest on his lips. "I'm not taking it back."

"You just said that it wasn't right."

"I'm not falling in love with you." He leans forward until his lips hover just over mine. "I love you."

I look into his eyes and I see all the truth that is within the words, in his eyes. "I love you too, Mr. Parker. I love you too."

Epilogue

One year later.

"Sooner or later, you're going to have to quit your job there and come back to work for me."

"Clive." I tap my hand over his. "I'm the director of new operations at Hughes. I'm not leaving my job."

"I can give you a fancy title and more money," he teases. "All you need to do is tell Alec that it's over and you're going to work for your husband."

I love hearing him say that. It's been only two months since we got married, but the knowledge that we are committed to one another forever still makes my heart skip a beat.

Our wedding had been intimate and beautiful. All the important people, in Clive's and now my life had been there with us. We married in Central Park at dusk. Cory had been the best man and Olivia had been my maid of honor. Technically, Sadie and Hunter had stood up for us. I'd taken a moment to hug Ben and toast to our mutual happiness. We've both come so far since we first met in the grief support group. Our lives crossing over in the most meaningful ways as our friendship has grown and blossomed to include our partners and friends.

"Do you want me to go get you some pickles and ice cream?"

I turn to look at my husband. The smile on his face radiates throughout every part of him. "I'm not craving anything tonight."

"Not even me?" He scoots his chair closer to where I'm sitting at the table.

I've spent every night this past month, organizing the old pictures that we brought to our condo from the storage facility. They are pictures of the family that I lost. I'm sorting through them, cataloguing them by date and event and placing the most special ones in albums.

"I'll show you how much I crave you later." I reach to cup his cheek in my palm. "I need you to help me with this for now."

"I'll do anything for my two beautiful girls." His hand settles on my swollen belly.

It's only another three months until our beautiful daughter, Haven, arrives. We've set up the nursery, bought more diapers than we'll ever need and picked out an outfit that we can bring her home from the hospital in.

She's named after my mother. Her name is a reflection of the woman who taught me about courage and grace.

"I can't wait until she gets here, Clive." I place my hand over his. "I can't wait to see if she has your beautiful eyes."

He nods slowly. "I want her to be just like you, Lilly."

"She'll be just like both of us."

"The world isn't ready for that yet." He chuckles.

"The world may not be." I lean towards him to graze my lips over his. "But I can't wait for the next chapter in our fairy tale to begin."

Preview of TRACE — The New Series

"There's a word for men like you." I try to sound as civilized as I can.

"Handsome?"

I look to the left to avoid eye contact with him. The man is devastatingly handsome. I can't say I'm surprised he realizes it. "No."

"Charming?"

I look at his face. He's smirking at me. He's actually standing in front of me, smirking. "No."

"Well-hung?" His gaze drops down to the front of the hospital gown he's wearing.

In instances like this I need to be professional. I'm a nurse. I'm a trained professional. If my eyes follow the path of his, there's no telling what I'm going to see. "No."

"You didn't even look," he teases. "Your eyes haven't left my face even though I'm here because I have a pain in my ass."

It's too easy. He's handing it right to me on a silver platter but I'm on duty so I can't react at all.

"Mr. Ryan." I glance down at the chart in my hand. "I get that you can't sit on the exam table because of the pain in your derriere, but you need to stay within this cubicle. Dr. Foster is going to be here shortly and if you're not here, it's just going to prolong the process."

"It's Garrett." His eyes settle on my nametag. "Vanessa, I'm in a lot of pain here."

"What exactly happened to you?" I already know the answer to this question. He crashed his bike and knocked himself out cold. It's worth hearing how he'll put a spin on it though. According to his chart he's a lawyer. Every lawyer I've ever known blurs the line between fact and fiction effortlessly.

"I was riding my bike in Central Park this morning." He shifts on his feet slightly. "I like to do that every morning to keep in shape."

"It's important to exercise." I don't look up from his chart.

"I was riding along and turned a corner and that's when I saw them." He shakes slightly.

If he falls over on my watch, I'm going to need to write up a report and I hate writing up reports. "Maybe you should lean against the stretcher."

He nods as he pushes his hand against it. "I was just riding along and I saw them, and after that everything went black."

"The paramedics that brought you in said you hit a tree." I wince at the image of that. "They said you were lucky you were wearing a helmet."

"I could have been luckier."

"How so?" I turn towards the curtain. Dr. Foster should have been in here by now. I'm going to need to find him.

"If I would have caught what I was chasing when I crashed, I would have been the luckiest guy in Manhattan."

"What were you chasing when you crashed?" I lean in waiting to hear the part of the story everyone in admitting has been dying to know. How does a grown man veer so far off the assigned bicycle path that he hits a huge tree head-on?

"I was chasing the most perfect pair of tits I've seen in a long time."

"Are you serious?" I lean closer to have a look at his eyes.

"I'm dead serious." His hands bolt to the air in front of him. "They were round and plump. She was jogging on the path and I saw them bounce and then they bounced again."

"That's just…" my voice trails because anything I want to say may result in my being suspended. Offending a patient is a definite no-no and I've already had two warnings. I only have one more before I'm out the door for good.

"I'm going to get Dr. Foster." The sooner we get this guy out of here the better.

"Her tits can't compare to your ass, Vanessa. It's seriously the best looking ass I've ever seen."

I can't resist. I know that there's a chance I'm going to regret this but I do it anyway. "No, I'd disagree with that."

"You can't." He shakes his head slightly even though it's the worst possible thing for him to do after slamming it into a tree. "I'm an ass man and your ass is the best looking one I've ever come across."

"Actually." I take a step closer to him. "You're the best looking ass I've ever come across. No, wait. That came out wrong."

He starts to turn to reveal his naked ass beneath the hospital gown he's been wearing since he arrived.

"I meant to say that you're an asshole," I spit out through clenched teeth.

"Nurse Meyer?"

I don't need to turn to recognize that voice. It's Dr. Foster. That one and only chance I had left just disappeared into thin air.

SOLO – *A Standalone by Deborah Bladon*

"Have you fucked anyone in the chorus?"

This is when I wish like hell I'd brought my ear buds with me. Listening to this guy try to pick up Claudia isn't my idea of the way to spend an elevator ride early on a Monday morning. You'd think that landing a part in a Broadway play would mean work, work, and more work. It wouldn't mean the incessant sexual undertones that drive through every rehearsal and meeting day-after-day.

"No," she replies calmly.

"I wasn't talking to you," he snaps. "You. I'm talking to you."

Considering there are only three of us riding this slow ass elevator to the fourteenth floor I guess I need to address this. "Me?" I turn to face him and I feel an instant need to find my balance. I rest my hand against the chrome bar that stretches along the walls of the lift. He's hot. Like smoking hot as hell hot. Why didn't I notice him when I got on?

"What's your name?"

"Libby." This is one of those moments when I wish my parents would have given more thought to what I'd feel like being a twenty-two-year-old woman carrying around the name of a four-year-old. Libby? I've hated the name since I was in grade school. It screams sweetness and light.

"Libby?" he repeats it back. "I like it."

"What's your name?" I try to sound somewhat invested in this. I know his type. I've met dozens of guys just like this since I've moved to Manhattan. He's looking for a quick fuck. He's wearing an incredibly expensive three-piece suit and cuff links that cost more than my first, and only, car. I wouldn't be surprised if most women fall to their knees in his presence and give him and his dick exactly what they want. It can't hurt that he's got the most intense green eyes I've ever seen and jet black hair that is tousled enough to make him look that much more irresistible.

"You didn't answer my question." He takes a heavy step towards me as more people enter the elevator on the third floor.

I push back into the chrome bar, the coolness of it seeping through my thin t-shirt. I almost wish I would have worn something nicer to the rehearsal hall. Who knew I'd end up face-to-face with this? "What question?"

"Have you fucked anyone in the chorus, Libby?" His voice is deep and intimate. It's too intimate for such a small, crowded place.

"That's none of your business." I inhale the scent of his cologne. It's luxurious, subtle and intoxicating.

His hand darts to my waist as more people join the most interesting elevator ride I've ever encountered. "It's more my business than you know."

I roll my hips away from him. I can't want this man. I can't let any man tear my attention away from my work. "I doubt that," I whisper. "I really doubt that."

"Don't doubt me, Libby." He pushes his body closer to mine, the unmistakable firm outline of his cock pressing against my stomach.

I breathe a heavy sigh of relief as the elevator finally chimes its arrival on the fourteenth floor. "This is my stop." I try to push past him, but his hand holds firm to my waist.

"It's mine too." His right hand jumps to the wall behind me, trapping me in place. "Allow me to formally introduce myself before you run off."

My eyes dart over his shoulder to where Claudia is throwing me a confused look as she exits the lift. "I need to go," I say. "I can't be late."

"Don't worry about being late. I'm Alec Hughes."

"You're Alec Hughes?" I feel my breath catch. "You're the investor. You own my play."

"Correction, Libby." He leans in closer until his lips are almost touching mine. "I own the play. You work for me."

Available now in Kindle Edition and Special Edition paperbacks.

Thank You!

Thank you for purchasing my book. I can't even begin to put to words what it means to me. If you enjoyed it, please remember to write a review for it. Let me know your thoughts! I want to keep my readers happy.

For more information on **The TRACE Series**, as well as updates, please visit my website, www.deborahbladon.com. There are book trailers and other goodies to check out.

If you want to chat with me personally, please LIKE my page on Facebook. I love connecting with all of my readers because without you, none of this would be possible. www.facebook.com/authordeborahbladon

Thank you, for everything.

About the Author

Deborah Bladon has never read a romance hero she didn't like. Her love for romance novels began when she was old enough to board the bus, library card in hand to check out the newest Harlequin paperbacks. She's a Canadian by heart, and by passport, but you can often spot her in New York City sipping a latte and looking for inspiration for her next story. Manhattan is definitely her second home.

She cherishes her family and believes that each day is a gift for writing, for reading, and for loving.

12978383R00125

Printed in Great Britain
by Amazon.co.uk, Ltd.,
Marston Gate.